"*THE WAY TO DUSTY DEATH* is vintage MacLean, which makes it very good indeed. . . . MacLean's account is taut, intense, and breath-taking. I don't know when I have read a better 'chase' sequence. Even if your appetite for thrillers is a bit jaded, I believe you will enjoy *THE WAY TO DUSTY DEATH*. It is quality entertainment."
—*SUNDAY WORLD-HERALD MAGAZINE*

"Wild entertainment in the MacLean style, written to entertain. It does."
—*LIBRARY JOURNAL*

"A seat-of-the-pants entertainment that never cruises at less than 100 miles per hour, and doesn't take more than two to read . . . Barely time to surface between action sequences."
—*KIRKUS REVIEWS*

"Tense excitement plunges at breakneck speed to a shattering climax. Add another high caliber adventure tale to the author's long list of chillers. The reader won't soon forget this race against death."
—*DELTA DEMOCRAT-TIMES*

"Filled with suspense, excitement, mystery, and danger, his story races along with headlong speed comparable to that of the cars he writes about."
—*BEST SELLERS*

THE WAY TO DUSTY DEATH

|||||||||||||||||||||||||||||||||||||||||||||||||||||||||||||||||||||||||||||||||

Alistair MacLean

A FAWCETT CREST BOOK

Fawcett Publications, Inc., Greenwich, Connecticut

THE WAY TO DUSTY DEATH

A Fawcett Crest Book reprinted by arrangement with Doubleday
and Company, Inc.

Library of Congress Catalog Card Number: 73-79870

Alternate Selection of the Literary Guild
Selection of the Bargain Book Club

Printed in the United States of America
September 1974

THE WAY TO
DUSTY DEATH

ONE

Harlow sat by the side of the race-track on that hot and cloudless afternoon, his long hair blowing about in the fresh breeze and partially obscuring his face, his golden helmet clutched so tightly in his gauntleted hands that he appeared to be trying to crush it: the hands were shaking uncontrollably and occasional violent tremors racked his entire body.

His own car, from which he had been miraculously thrown clear, uninjured just before it had overturned, lay, of all places, in its own Coronado pits, upside down and with its wheels spinning idly. Wisps of smoke were coming from an engine already engulfed under a mound of foam from the fire extinguishers and it was clear that there was now little danger left of an explosion from the unruptured fuel tanks.

Alexis Dunnet, the first to reach Harlow, noticed that he wasn't looking at his own car but was staring, trance-like, at a spot about two hundred yards further along the track where an already dead man called Isaac Jethou was being cremated in the white-flamed funeral pyre of what had once been his Grand Prix Formula One racing car. There was curiously little smoke coming from the blazing wreck, presumably because of the intense heat given off by the incandescent magnesium alloy wheels, and when the gusting wind occasionally parted the towering curtains of flame Jethou could be seen sitting bolt upright in his cockpit, the one apparently undamaged structure left in an otherwise shattered and unrecognisable mass of twisted steel: at least Dunnet *knew* it was Jethou but what he was seeing was a blackened and horribly charred remnant of a human being.

The many thousands of people in the stands and lining the track were motionless and soundless, staring in transfixed and incredulous awe and horror at the burning car. The last of the engines of the Grand Prix cars—there were nine of them stopped in sight of the pits, some drivers standing by their sides—died away as the race marshals frantically flagged the abandonment of the race.

The public address system had fallen silent now, as did a siren's undulating wail as an ambulance screeched to a halt at a prudent distance from Jethou's car, its flashing light fading into nothingness against the white blaze in the background. Rescue workers in aluminum asbestos suits, some operating giant wheeled fire extinguishers, some armed with crowbars and axes, were trying desperately, for some reason wholly beyond the bounds of logic, to get sufficiently close to the car to drag the cindered corpse free, but the undiminished intensity of the flames made a mockery of their desperation. Their efforts were as futile as the presence of the ambulance was unnecessary. Jethou was beyond any mortal help or hope.

Dunnet looked away and down at the overalled figure beside him. The hands that held the golden helmet still trembled unceasingly and the eyes still fixed immovably on the sheeted flames that now quite enveloped Isaac Jethou's car were the eyes of an eagle gone blind. Dunnet reached for his shoulder and shook it gently but he paid no heed. Dunnet asked him if he were hurt for his face and trembling hands were masked in blood; he had cartwheeled at least half-a-dozen times after being thrown from his car in the final moments before it had upended and come to rest in its own pits. Harlow stirred and looked at Dunnet, blinking, like a man slowly arousing himself from a nightmare, then shook his head.

Two ambulance men with a stretcher came towards them at a dead run, but Harlow, unaided except for Dunnet's supporting hand under his upper arm, pushed himself shakily to his feet and waved them off. He didn't, however, seem to object to what little help Dunnet's hand lent him and they walked slowly back to the Coronado pits, the still dazed and virtually uncomprehending Harlow; Dunnet tall, thin, with dark hair parted in the middle, a dark pencil-line moustache and rimless glasses, everyone's idealised conception of a city accountant even although his passport declared him to be a journalist.

MacAlpine, a fire extinguisher still held in one hand, turned to meet them at the entrance to the pits. James MacAlpine, owner and manager of the Coronado racing team, dressed in a now-stained tan gaberdine suit, was in his mid-fifties, as heavily jowled as he was heavily built with a deeply lined face under an impressive mane of black and silver hair. Behind him, Jacobson, the chief mechanic, and his two red-haired assistants, the Rafferty twins, who for some reason unknown were invariably referred to as Tweedledum and Tweedledee, still ministered to the smouldering Coronado while behind the car two other men, white-coated first-aid men, were carrying out more serious ministrations of their own: on the ground, unconscious but still clutching the pad and pencil with which she had been taking lap times, lay Mary MacAlpine, the owner's black-haired twenty-year-old daughter. The first-aid men were bent over her left leg and scissoring open to the knee wine-red slacks that had been white moments ago. MacAlpine took Harlow's arm, deliberately shielding him from the sight of his daughter, and led him to the little shelter behind the pits. MacAlpine was an extremely able, competent and tough man, as millionaires tend to be: beneath the toughness, as of now, lay a kindness and depth of consideration of which no one would have dared to accuse him.

In the back of the shelter stood a small wooden crate which was, in effect, a portable bar. Most of it was given over to an ice-box stocked with a little beer and lots of soft drinks, chiefly for the mechanics, for working under that torrid sun was thirsty business. There were also two bottles of champagne for it had not been unreasonable to expect of a man who had just reeled off a near-impossible five consecutive Grand Prix victories that he might just possibly achieve his sixth. Harlow opened the lid of the crate, ignored the ice-box, lifted out a bottle of brandy and half-filled the tumbler, the neck of the bottle chattering violently against the rim of the glass: more brandy spilled to the ground than went into the glass. He required both hands to lift the glass to his mouth and now the rim of the tumbler, castanet-like fashion, struck up an even more erratic tattoo against his teeth than the bottle had on the glass. He managed to get some of it down but most of the glass's contents overflowed by the two sides of his mouth, coursed down the blood-streaked chin to stain the white racing overalls to exactly the same

11

colour as the slacks of the injured girl outside. Harlow stared bemusedly at the empty glass, sank on to a bench and reached for the bottle again.

MacAlpine looked at Dunnet, his face without expression. Harlow had suffered three major crashes in his racing career, in the last of which, two years previously, he had sustained near-fatal injuries: on that last occasion, he had been smiling, albeit in agony, as his stretcher had been loaded aboard the ambulance plane for the flight back to London and the left hand he had used to give the thumbs-up signal—his right forearm had been broken in two places—had been as steady as if graven from marble. But more dismaying was the fact that apart from a token sip of celebration champagne, he had never touched hard alcohol in his life.

It happens to them all, MacAlpine had always maintained, sooner or later it happens to them all. No matter how cool or brave or brilliant they were, it happened to them all, and the more steely their icy calm and control the more fragile it was. MacAlpine was never a man to be averse to the odd hyperbolic turn of phrase and there was a handful—but only a handful—of outstanding ex Grand Prix drivers around who had retired at the top of their physical and mental form, sufficient, at any rate, to disprove MacAlpine's statement in its entirety. But it was well enough known that there existed top-flight drivers who had crashed or who had suffered so much nervous and mental fatigue that they had become empty shells of their former selves, that

there were among the current twenty-four Grand
Prix drivers four or five who would never win a race
again because they had no intention of ever trying
to do so, who kept going only in order to shore up
the façade of a now empty pride. But there are some
things that are not done in the racing world and one
of those is that you don't remove a man from the
Grand Prix roster just because his nerve is gone.

But that MacAlpine was more often right than
wrong was sadly clear from the sight of that
trembling figure hunched on the bench. If ever a
man had gone over the top, had reached and passed
the limit of endurance before tumbling over the
precipice of self-abnegation and hapless acceptance
of ultimate defeat, it was Johnny Harlow, the gold-
en boy of the Grand Prix circuits, unquestionably,
until that afternoon, the outstanding driver of his
time and, it was being increasingly suggested, of all
time: with last year's world championship safely his
and the current year's, by any reasonable standards,
almost inevitably his with half the Grand Prix races
still to run, Harlow's will and nerve would have appeared to have crumbled beyond recovery: it was
plain to both MacAlpine and Dunnet that the
charred being who had been Isaac Jethou would
haunt him for however long his days were to be.

Not that the signs hadn't been there before for
those with eyes to see them and most of the drivers
and mechanics on the circuits had the kind of eyes
that were required. Ever since the second Grand
Prix race of the season, which he had easily and

convincingly won unaware of the fact that his brilliant younger brother had been forced off the track and had telescoped his car into a third of its length against the base of a pine tree at something over a hundred and fifty miles an hour, the signs had been there. Never a sociable or gregarious person, he had become increasingly withdrawn, increasingly taciturn, and when he smiled, and it was rarely, it was the empty smile of a man who could find nothing in life to smile about. Normally the most icily calculating and safety-conscious of drivers, his impeccable standards had become eroded and his previous near-obsession with safety dismayingly decreased while, contradictorily, he had consistently kept on breaking lap records on circuits throughout Europe. But he had continued on his record-breaking way, capturing one Grand Prix trophy after the other at the increasingly mounting expense of himself and his fellow competitors: his driving had become reckless and increasingly dangerous and the other drivers, tough and hardened professionals though they all were, began to go in fear of him for instead of disputing a corner with him as they would normally have done they had nearly all of them fallen into the habit of pulling well in when they saw his lime-green Coronado closing up on their driving mirrors. This, in all conscience, was seldom enough, for Harlow had an extremely simple race-winning formula—to get in front and stay there.

By now more and more people were saying out loud that his suicidally competitive driving on the race-tracks signified not a battle against his peers but a battle against himself. It had become increasingly obvious, latterly painfully obvious, that this was one battle that he would never win, that this last-ditch stand against his failing nerve could have only one end, that one day his luck would run out. And so it had, and so had Isaac Jethou's, and Johnny Harlow, for all the world to see, had lost his last battle on the Grand Prix tracks of Europe and America. Maybe he would move out on the tracks again, maybe he would start fighting again: but it seemed certain then that no one knew with more dreadful clarity than Harlow that his fighting days were over.

For a third time Harlow reached out for the neck of the brandy bottle, his hands as unsteady as ever. The once-full bottle was now one-third empty but only a fraction of that had found its way down his throat, so uncontrollable were his movements. MacAlpine looked gravely at Dunnet, shrugged his heavy shoulders in a gesture of either resignation or acceptance and then glanced out into the pits. An ambulance had just arrived for his daughter and as MacAlpine hurried out Dunnet set about cleaning up Harlow's face with the aid of a sponge and a bucket of water. Harlow didn't seem to care one way or another whether his face was washed: whatever his thoughts were, and in the circumstances it would have taken an idiot not to read them aright, his entire attention appeared to be concentrated on the contents of that bottle of Martell, the picture of

a man, if ever there was one, who desperately need-
ed and urgently sought immediate oblivion.

It was as well, perhaps, that both Harlow and
MacAlpine failed to notice a person standing just
outside the door whose expression clearly indicated
that he would have taken quite some pleasure in as-
sisting Harlow into a state of permanent oblivion.
Rory, MacAlpine's son, a dark curly-haired youth
of a normally amiable, even sunny, disposition, had
now a dark thundercloud on his face, an unthinkable expression for one who for years, and until
only a few minutes previously, regarded Harlow as
the idol of his life. Rory looked away towards the
ambulance where his unconscious and blood-
soaked sister lay and then the unthinkable was no
longer so. He turned again to look at Harlow and
now the emotion reflected in his eyes was as close to
outright hatred as a sixteen-year-old was ever likely to achieve.

The official enquiry into the cause of the accident, held almost immediately afterwards, predictably failed to indict any one man as the sole cause
of the disaster. Official race enquiries almost never
did, including the notorious enquiry into that un-
paralleled Le Mans holocaust when seventy-three
spectators were killed and no one was found to
blame whereas it was common knowledge at the
time that one man and one man only—dead now
these many years—had been the person responsible
for it.

This particular enquiry failed to indict, in spite of

the fact that two or three thousand people in the main stands would have unhesitatingly laid the sole charge at the door of Johnny Harlow. But even more damning was the incontrovertible evidence supplied in the small hall where the enquiry was held by a TV playback of the entire incident. The projection screen had been small and stained but the picture clear enough and the sound effects all too vivid and true to life. In the rerun of the film— it lasted barely twenty seconds but was screened five times—three Grand Prix cars, viewed from the rear but being closely followed by the telescopic zoom lens, could be seen approaching the pits. Harlow, in his Coronado, was closing up on the leading car, a vintage privately entered Ferrari that was leading only by virtue of the fact that it had already lost a lap. Moving even more quickly than Harlow and well clear on the other side of the track was a works-entered fire-engine-red Ferrari driven by a brilliant Californian, Isaac Jethou. In the straight Jethou's twelve cylinders had a considerable edge over Harlow's eight and it was clear that he intended to pass. It seemed that Harlow, too, was quite aware of this for his brake lights came on in keeping with his apparent intention of easing slightly and tucking in behind the slower car while Jethou swept by.

Suddenly, incredibly, Harlow's brake lights went out and the Coronado swerved violently outwards as if Harlow had decided he could overtake the car in front before Jethou could overtake him. If that had been his inexplicable intention then it had been the most foolhardy of his life, for he had taken his car directly into the path of Isaac Jethou, who, on that straight, could not have been travelling at less than 180 miles an hour and who, in the fraction of the second available to him had never even the most remote shadow of a chance to take the only braking or avoiding action that could have saved him.

At the moment of impact, Jethou's front wheel struck squarely into the side of Harlow's front wheel. For Harlow the consequences of the collision were, in all conscience, serious enough for it sent his car into an uncontrollable spin, but for Jethou they were disastrous. Even above the cacophonous clamour of engines under maximum revolutions and the screeching of locked tyres on the tarmac, the bursting of Jethou's front tyre was heard as a rifle shot and from that instant Jethou was a dead man. His Ferrari, wholly out of control and now no more than a mindless mechanical monster bent on its own destruction, smashed into and caromed off the nearside safety barrier and, already belching gouts of red flame and black oily smoke, careered wildly across the track to strike the far-side barrier, rear end first, at a speed of still over a hundred miles an hour. The Ferrari, spinning wildly, slid down the track for about two hundred yards, turned over twice and came to rest on all four wrecked wheels, Jethou still trapped in the cockpit but even then almost certainly dead. It was then that the red flames turned to white.

That Harlow had been directly responsible for

Jethou's death was beyond dispute but Harlow, with eleven Grand Prix wins behind him in seventeen months, was, by definition and on his record, the best driver in the world and one simply does not indict the best driver in the world. It is not the done thing. The whole tragic affair was attributed to the race-track equivalent of an Act of God and the curtain was discreetly lowered to indicate the end of the act.

TWO

|||||||||||||||||||||||

The French, even at their most relaxed and unemotional, are little given to hiding their feelings and the packed crowd at Clermont-Ferrand that day, which was notably unrelaxed and highly emotional, was in no mood to depart from their Latin norm. As Harlow, head bowed, trudged rather than walked along the side of the racetrack from the court of enquiry towards the Coronado pits, they became very vocal indeed. Their booing, hissing, cat-calling and just plain shouts of anger, accompanied by much Gallic waving of clenched fists, were as threatening as they were frightening. Not only was it an ugly

scene, it was one that looked as if it would only require one single flash-point to trigger off a near-riot,
to convert their vengeful emotions towards Johnny
Harlow into physical action against him and this, it
was clear, was the apprehension that was uppermost
in the minds of the police, for they moved in close to
afford Harlow such protection as he might require.
It was equally clear from the expressions on their
faces that the police did not relish their task, and
from the way they averted their faces from Harlow
that they sympathised with their countrymen's feelings.

A few paces behind Harlow, flanked by Dunnet
and MacAlpine, walked another man who clearly
shared the opinions of police and spectators. Angrily twirling his racing helmet by his strap, he was
clad in racing overalls identical to those that Harlow
was wearing: Nicola Tracchia was, in fact, the No. 2
driver in the Coronado racing team. Tracchia was
almost outrageously handsome, with dark curling
hair, a gleaming perfection of teeth that no denti-
frice manufacturer would ever dare use as an adver-
tisement and a sun-tan that would have turned a life-
guard pale green. That he wasn't looking particularly happy at that moment was directly attributable
to the fact that he was scowling heavily: the legen-
dary Tracchia scowl was a memorable thing of
wonder, in constant use and held in differing degrees of respect, awe and downright fear but never
ignored. Tracchia had a low opinion of his fellow-

man and regarded the majority of people, and this with particular reference to his fellow-Grand Prix drivers, as retarded adolescents.

Understandably, he operated in a limited social circle. What made matters worse for Tracchia was his realisation that, brilliant driver though he was, he was fractionally less good than Harlow; and even this was exacerbated by the knowledge that, no matter how long or desperately he tried, he would never quite close that fractional gap. When he spoke now to MacAlpine he made no effort to lower his voice, which in the circumstances mattered not at all for Harlow could not possibly have heard him above the baying of the crowd: but it was quite clear that Tracchia would not have lowered his voice no matter what the circumstances.

"An Act of God!" The bitter incredulity in the voice was wholly genuine. "Jesus Christ! Did you hear what those cretins called it? An Act of God! An act of murder, I call it."

"No, lad, no." MacAlpine put his hand on Tracchia's shoulder, only to have it angrily shrugged off. MacAlpine sighed. "At the very outside, manslaughter. And not even that. You know yourself how many Grand Prix drivers have died in the past four years because their cars went wild."

"Wild! Wild!" Tracchia, at a momentary and most uncharacteristic loss for words, gazed heavenwards in silent appeal. "Good God, Mac, we all saw it on the screen. We saw it five times. He took his foot off the brake and pulled out straight in front of Jethou. An Act of God! Sure, sure, sure. It's an Act of God because he's won eleven Grand Prix in seventeen months, because he won last year's championship and looks as if he's going to do the same this year."

"What do you mean?"

"You know damn well what I mean. Take him off the tracks and you might as well take us all off the tracks. He's the champion, isn't he? If he's that bad, then what the hell must the rest of us be like? We know that's not the case, but will the public? Will they hell. God knows that there are already too many people, and damned influential people as well, agitating that Grand Prix racing should be banned throughout the world, and too many countries just begging for a good excuse to get out. This would be the excuse of a lifetime. We *need* our Johnny Harlows, don't we, Mac? Even though they do go around killing people."

"I thought he was your friend, Nikki?"

"Sure, Mac. Sure he's my friend. So was Jethou."

There was no reply for MacAlpine to make to this so he made none. Tracchia appeared to have said his say, for he fell silent and got back to his scowling. In silence and in safety—the police escort had been steadily increasing—the four men reached the Coronado pits. Without a glance at or word to anyone Harlow made for the little shelter at the rear of the pits. In their turn nobody—Jacobson and his two mechanics were there also—made any attempt to speak to or stop him, nor did any among them do even as much as trouble to exchange significant glances: the starkly obvious requires no emphasis. Jacobson ignored him entirely and came up to Mac-Alpine. The chief mechanic—and he was one of acknowledged genius—was a lean, tall and strongly built man. He had a dark and deeply lined face that looked as if it hadn't smiled for a long time and wasn't about to make an exception in this case either.

He said: "Harlow's clear, of course."

"Of course? I don't understand."

"*I* have to tell *you?* Indict Harlow and you set the sport back ten years. Too many millions tied up in it to allow that to happen. Isn't there now, Mr Mac-Alpine?"

MacAlpine looked at him reflectively, not answering, glanced briefly at the still scowling Tracchia, turned away and walked across to Harlow's battered and fire-blistered Coronado, which was by that time back on all four wheels. He examined it leisurely, almost contemplatively, stooped over the cockpit, turned the steering wheel, which offered no resistance to his hand, then straightened.

He said: "Well, now. I wonder."

Jacobson looked at him coldly. His eyes, expressing displeasure, could be as formidable and intimidating as Tracchia's scowl. He said: "*I* prepared that car, Mr MacAlpine."

MacAlpine's shoulders rose and fell in a long moment of silence.

"I know, Jacobson, I know. I also know you're

the best in the business. I also know that you've been too long in it to talk nonsense. *Any* car can go. How long?"

"You want me to start now?"

"That's it."

"Four hours." Jacobson was curt, offence given and taken. "Six at the most."

MacAlpine nodded, took Dunnet by the arm, prepared to walk away then halted. Tracchia and Rory were together talking in low indistinct voices but their words didn't have to be understood, the rigid hostility in their expressions as they looked at Harlow and his bottle of brandy inside the hut was eloquent enough. MacAlpine, his hand still on Dunnet's arm, moved away and sighed again.

"Johnny's not making too many friends today, is he?"

"He hasn't been for far too many days. And I think that here's another friend that he's about not to make."

"Oh, Jesus." Sighs seemed to be becoming second nature to MacAlpine. "Neubauer does seem to have something on his mind."

The figure in sky-blue racing overalls striding towards the pits did indeed seem to have something on his mind. Neubauer was tall, very blond and completely Nordic in appearance although he was in fact Austrian. The No. 1 driver for team Cagliari —he had the word *Cagliari* emblazoned across the chest of his overalls—his consistent brilliance on the Grand Prix tracks had made him the acknowledged crown prince of racing and Harlow's eventual and inevitable successor. Like Tracchia, he was a cool, distant man wholly incapable of standing fools at any price, far less gladly. Like Tracchia, his friends and intimates were restricted to a very small group indeed: it was matter for neither wonder nor speculation that those two men, the most unforgiving of rivals on the race-tracks, were, off-track, close friends.

Neubauer, with compressed lips and cold pale-blue eyes glittering, was clearly a very angry man and his humour wasn't improved when MacAlpine moved his massive bulk to block his way. Neubauer had no option other than to stop: big man though he was MacAlpine was very much bigger. When he spoke it was with his teeth clamped together.

"Out of my way."

MacAlpine looked at him in mild surprise.

"You said what?"

"Sorry, Mr MacAlpine. Where's that bastard Harlow?"

"Leave him be. He's not well."

"And Jethou is, I suppose? I don't know who the hell or what the hell Harlow is or is supposed to be and I don't care. Why should that maniac get off scot-free. He *is* a maniac. You know it. We all know it. He forced me off the road twice today, that could just as well have been me burnt to death as Jethou. I'm giving you warning, Mr. MacAlpine. I'm going to call a meeting of the G.P.D.A. and have him banned from the circuits."

"You're the last person who can afford to do that, Willi." MacAlpine put his hands on Neubauer's shoulders. "The last person who can afford to put the finger on Johnny. If Harlow goes, who's the next champion?"

Neubauer stared at him. Some of the fury left his face and he stared at MacAlpine in almost bewildered disbelief. When his voice came it was low, almost an uncertain whisper. "You think I would do it for that, Mr MacAlpine?"

"No, Willi, I don't. I'm just pointing out that most others would."

There was a long pause during which what was left of Neubauer's anger died away. He said quietly: "He's a killer. He'll kill again." Gently, he removed MacAlpine's hands, turned and left the pits. Thoughtfully, worriedly, Dunnet watched him leave.

"He could be right, James. Sure, sure, he's won four Grand Prix in a row but ever since his brother was killed in the Spanish Grand Prix—well, you know."

"Four Grand Prix under his belt and you're trying to tell me that his nerve is gone?"

"I don't know what's gone. I just don't know. All I know is that the safest driver on the circuits has become so reckless and dangerous, so suicidally competitive if you like, that the other drivers are just plain scared of him. As far as they are concerned, the freedom of the road is his, they'd rather

27

live than dispute a yard of track with him. *That's*
why he keeps on winning."

MacAlpine regarded Dunnet closely and shook
his head in unease. He, MacAlpine, and not Dunnet, was the acknowledged expert, but MacAlpine
held both Dunnet and his opinions in the highest regard. Dunnet was an extraordinarily shrewd, intelli-
gent and able person. He was a journalist by profes-
sion, and a highly competent one, who had switched
from being a political analyst to a sports commenta-
tor for the admittedly unarguable reason that there
is no topic on earth so irretrievably dull as politics.
The acute penetration and remarkable powers of
observation and analysis that had made him so formidable a figure on the Westminster scene he had
transferred easily and successfully to the race-tracks
of the world. A regular correspondent for a British
national daily and two motoring magazines, one
British, one American—although he did a remarkable amount of free-lance work on the side—he
had rapidly established himself as one of the very
few really outstanding motor racing journalists in
the world. To do this in the space of just over two
years had been a quite outstanding achievement by
any standard. So successful had he been, indeed,
that he had incurred the envy and displeasure, not
to say the outright wrath, of a considerable number
of his less gifted peers.

Nor was their minimal regard for him in any way
heightened by what they sourly regarded as the lim-
petlike persistency with which he had attached him-

self to the Coronado team on an almost permanent basis. Not that there were any laws, written or un-written, about this sort of behaviour, for no independent journalist had ever done this sort of thing before. Now that it had been done it was, his fellow-writers said, a thing that simply was not done. It was his job, they maintained and com-plained, to write in a fair and unbiased fashion on *all* the cars and *all* the drivers in the Grand Prix field and their resentment remained undiminished when he pointed out to them, reasonably and with unchallengeable accuracy, that this was precisely what he did. What really grieved them, of course, was that he had the inside track on the Coronado team, then the fastest burgeoning and most glamor-ous race company in the business: and it would have been difficult to deny that the number of off-track articles he had written partly about the team but primarily about Harlow would have made up a pretty fair-sized volume. Nor had matters been helped by the existence of a book on which he had collaborated with Harlow.

MacAlpine said: "I'm afraid you're right, Alexis. Which means that I know you're right but I don't even want to admit it to myself. He's just terrifying the living daylights out of everyone. And out of me. And now this."

They looked across the pits to where Harlow was sitting on a bench just outside the shelter. Uncaring whether he was observed or not, he half-filled a glass from a rapidly diminishing brandy bottle. One

did not have to have eyesight to know that the
hands were still shaking: diminishing though the
protesting roar of the crowd still was, it was still sufficient to make normal conversation difficult: nevertheless, the castanet rattle of glass against glass
could be clearly heard. Harlow took a quick gulp
from his glass then sat there with both elbows on his
knees and stared, unblinkingly and without expression, at the wrecked remains of his car.

Dunnet said: "And only two months ago he'd
never touched the hard stuff in his life. What are
you going to do, James?"

"Now?" MacAlpine smiled faintly. "I'm going to
see Mary. I think by this time they might let me see
her." He glanced briefly, his face seemingly impassive, around the pits, at Harlow lifting his glass
again, at the redhaired Rafferty twins looking almost as unhappy as Dunnet, and at Jacobson, Tracchia and Rory wearing uniform scowls and direct-
ing them in uniform directions, sighed for the last
time, turned and walked heavily away.

Mary MacAlpine was twenty years old, pale-
complexioned despite the many hours she spent in
the sun, with big brown eyes, gleamingly brushed
black hair as dark as night and the most bewitching
smile that ever graced a Grand Prix racing track:
she did not intend that the smile should be bewitching, she just couldn't help it. Everyone in the team,
even the taciturn and terrible-tempered Jacobson,
was in love with her in one way or another, not to
mention a quite remarkable number of other people

who were not in the team: this Mary recognised and accepted with commendable aplomb, although without either amusement or condescension: condescension was quite alien to her nature. In any event, she viewed the regard that others had for her as only the natural reciprocal of the regard she had for them: despite her quick no-nonsense mind, Mary MacAlpine was in many ways still very young.

Lying in bed in that spotless, soullessly antiseptic hospital room that night, Mary MacAlpine looked younger than ever. She also looked, as she unquestionably was, very ill. The natural paleness had turned to pallor and the big brown eyes, which she opened only briefly and reluctantly, were dulled with pain. This same pain was reflected in MacAlpine's eyes as he looked down at his daughter, at the heavily splinted and bandaged left leg lying on top of the sheet. MacAlpine stooped and kissed his daughter on the forehead.

He said: "Sleep well, darling. Goodnight."

She tried to smile. "With all the pills they've given me? Yes, I think I will. And Daddy."

"Darling?"

"It wasn't Johnny's fault. I know it wasn't. It was his car. I know it was."

"We're finding that out. Jacobson is taking the car down."

"You'll see. Will you ask Johnny to come and see me?"

"Not tonight, darling. I'm afraid he's not too well."

"He—he hasn't been—"

"No, no. Shock." MacAlpine smiled. "He's been fed the same pills as yourself."

"Johnny Harlow? In shock? I don't believe it. Three near-fatal crashes and he never once—"

"He saw you, my darling." He squeezed her hand. "I'll be around later tonight."

MacAlpine left the room and walked down to the reception area. A doctor was speaking to the nurse at the desk. He had grey hair, tired eyes and the face of an aristocrat. MacAlpine said: "Are you the person who is looking after my daughter?"

"Mr MacAlpine? Yes, I am. Dr Chollet."

"She seems very ill."

"No, Mr MacAlpine. No problem. She is just under heavy sedation. For the pain, you understand."

"I see. How long will she be—"

"Two weeks. Perhaps three. No more."

"One question, Dr Chollet. Why is her leg not in traction?"

"It would seem, Mr MacAlpine, that you are not a man who is afraid of the truth."

"Why is her leg not in traction?"

"Traction is for broken bones, Mr MacAlpine. Your daughter's left ankle bone, I'm afraid, is not just broken, it is—how would you say it in English? —pulverised, yes, I think that is the word, pulverised beyond any hope of remedial surgery. What's left of the bone will have to be fused together."

"Meaning that she can never bend her ankle

again?" Chollet inclined his head. "A permanent limp? For life?"

"You can have a second opinion, Mr MacAlpine. The best orthopaedic specialist in Paris. You are entitled—"

"No. That will not be necessary. The truth is obvious, Dr Chollet. One accepts the obvious."

"I am deeply sorry, Mr MacAlpine. She is a lovely child. But I am only a surgeon. Miracles? No. No miracles."

"Thank you, Doctor. You are most kind. I'll be back in about say—two hours?"

"Please not. She will be asleep for at least twelve hours. Perhaps sixteen."

MacAlpine nodded his head in acceptance and left.

Dunnet pushed away his plate with his untouched meal, looked at MacAlpine's plate, similarly untouched, then at the brooding MacAlpine.

He said: "I don't think either of us, James, is as tough as we thought we were."

"Age, Alexis. It overtakes us all."

"Yes. And at very high speed, it would seem." Dunnet pulled his plate towards him, regarded it sorrowfully then pushed it away again.

"Well, I suppose it's a damn sight better than amputation."

"There's that. There's that." MacAlpine pushed back his chair. "A walk, I think, Alexis."

"For the appetite? It won't work. Not with me."

"Nor with me. I just thought it might be interesting to see if Jacobson has turned up anything."

The garage was very long, low, heavily skylighted, brilliantly lit with hanging spotlights and, for a garage, was remarkably clean and tidy. Jacobson was at the inner end, stooped over Harlow's wrecked Coronado, when the metal door screeched open. He straightened, acknowledged the presence of MacAlpine and Dunnet with a wave of his hand, then returned to his examination of the car.

Dunnet closed the door and said quietly: "Where are the other mechanics?"

MacAlpine said: "You should know by this time. Jacobson always works alone on a crash job. A very low opinion of other mechanics, has Jacobson. Says they either overlook·evidence or destroy it by clumsiness."

The two men advanced and watched in silence as Jacobson tightened a connection in a hydraulic brake line. They were not alone in watching him. Directly above them, through an open skylight, the powerful lamps in the garage reflected on something metallic. The metallic object was a hand-held eight-millimetre camera and the hands that held them were very steady indeed. They were the hands of Johnny Harlow. His face was as impassive as his hands were motionless, intent and still and totally watchful. It was also totally sober.

MacAlpine said: "Well?"

Jacobson straightened and tenderly massaged an obviously aching back.

"Nothing. Just nothing. Supension, brakes, engine, transmission, tyres, steering—all O.K."

"But the steering—"

"Sheared. Impact fracture. Couldn't be anything else. It was still working when he pulled out in front of Jethou. You can't tell me that the steering suddenly went in that one second of time, Mr MacAlpine. Coincidence is coincidence, but that would be just a bit too much."

Dunnet said: "So we're still in the dark?"

"It's broad daylight where I stand. The oldest reason in the business. Driver error."

"Driver error." Dunnet shook his head. "Johnny Harlow never made a driver error in his life."

Jacobson smiled, his eyes cold. "I'd like to have the opinion of Jethou's ghost on that one."

MacAlpine said: "This hardly helps. Come on. Hotel. You haven't even eaten yet, Jacobson." He looked at Dunnet. "A night-cap in the bar, I think, then a look-in on Johnny."

Jacobson said: "You'll be wasting your time, sir. He'll be paralytic."

MacAlpine looked at Jacobson consideringly, then said very slowly and after a long pause: "He's still world champion. He's still Coronado's number one."

"So that's the way of it, is it?"

"You want it some other way?"

Jacobson crossed to a sink, began to wash his hands. Without turning he said: "You're the boss, Mr MacAlpine."

MacAlpine made no reply. When Jacobson had dried his hands the three men left the garage in silence, closing the heavy metal door behind them.

Only the top half of Harlow's head and supporting hands were visible as he clung to the ridge-pole of the garage's V-roof and watched the three men walk up the brightly lit main street. As soon as they had turned a corner and disappeared from sight, he slid gingerly down towards the opened skylight, lowered himself through the opening and felt with his feet until he found a metal cross-beam. He released his grip on the skylight sill, balanced precariously on the beam, brought out a small flashlight from an inner pocket—Jacobson had switched off all the lights before leaving—and directed it downwards. The concrete floor was about nine feet below him.

Harlow stooped, reached for the beam with his hands, slid down over it, hung at the full stretch of his hands then released his grip. He landed lightly and easily, headed for the door, switched on all the lights then went directly to the Coronado. He was carrying not one but two strap-hung cameras, his eight-millimetre cine and a very compact still camera with flashlight attachment.

He found an oily cloth and used it to rub clean part of the right suspension, a fuel line, the steering linkage and one of the carburetors in the engine compartment. Each of these areas he flash-photographed several times with the still camera. He retrieved the cloth, coated it with a mixture of oil and dirt from the floor, swiftly smeared the parts he had photographed and threw the cloth into a metal bin provided for that purpose.

He crossed to the door and tugged on the handle, but to no avail. The door had been locked from the outside and its heavy construction precluded any thought or attempt to force it: and Harlow's last thought was to leave any trace of his passing. He looked quickly round the garage.

On his left hand side was a light wooden ladder suspended from two right-angle wall brackets—a ladder almost certainly reserved for the cleaning of the very considerable skylight area. Below it, and to one side, lay, in a corner, the untidy coil of a tow-rope.

Harlow moved to the corner, picked up the rope, lifted the ladder off its brackets, looped the rope round the top rung and placed the ladder against the metal cross-beam. He returned to the door and switched off the lights. Using his flashlight, he climbed up the ladder and straddled the beam. Grasping the ladder while still maintaining his grip on the rope, he manoeuvred the former until the lower end hooked on to one of the right-angle wall brackets. Using the looped rope, he lowered the other end of the ladder until, not without some difficulty, he managed to drop it into the other bracket. He released one end of the rope, pulled it clear of the ladder, coiled it up and threw it into the corner where it had been previously lying. Then, swaying dangerously, he managed to bring himself upright on the beam, thrust himself head and shoulders through the opened skylight, hauled himself up and disappeared into the night above.

MacAlpine and Dunnet were seated alone at a table in an otherwise deserted lounge bar. They were seated in silence as a waiter brought them two scotches. MacAlpine raised his glass and smiled without humour.

"When you come to the end of a perfect day. God, I'm tired."

"So you're committed, James. So Harlow goes on."

"Thanks to Jacobson. Didn't leave me much option, did he?"

Harlow, running along the brightly lit main street, stopped abruptly. The street was almost entirely deserted except for two tall men approaching his way. Harlow hesitated, looked around swiftly, then pressed into a deeply recessed shop entrance. He stood there immobile as the two men passed by: they were Nicola Tracchia, Harlow's team-mate, and Willi Neubauer, engrossed in low-voiced and clearly very earnest conversation. Neither of them saw Harlow. They passed by. Harlow emerged from the recessed doorway, looked cautiously both ways, waited until the retreating backs of Tracchia and

Neubauer had turned a corner, then broke into a run again.

MacAlpine and Dunnet drained their glasses. MacAlpine looked questioningly at Dunnet. Dunnet said: "Well, I suppose we've got to face it sometime."

MacAlpine said: "I suppose." Both men rose, nodded to the barman and left.

Harlow, now moving at no more than a fast walk, crossed the street in the direction of a neon-signed hotel. Instead of using the main entrance, he went down a side alley-way, turned to his right and started to climb a fire-escape two steps at a time. His steps were as surefooted as a mountain goat's, his balance immaculate, his face registering no emotion. Only his eyes registered any expression. They were clear and still but possessed an element of concentrated calculation. It was the face of a dedicated man who knew completely what he was about.

MacAlpine and Dunnet were outside a door, numbered 412. MacAlpine's face registered a peculiar mixture of anger and concern. Dunnet's face, oddly, showed only unconcern. It could have been tight-lipped unconcern, but then Dunnet was habitually a tight-lipped man. MacAlpine hammered loudly on the door. The hammering brought no reaction. MacAlpine glanced furiously at his bruising knuckles, glanced at Dunnet and started a renewed assault on the door. Dunnet had no comment to make, either vocally or facially.

Harlow reached a platform on the fourth-floor fire-escape. He swung over the guard-railing, took a long step towards a nearby open window, negotiated the crossing safely and passed inside. The room was small. A suitcase lay on the floor, its contents spilled out in considerable disarray. On the bedside table stood a low-wattage lamp, which gave the only weak illumination in the room, and a half-empty bottle of whisky. Harlow closed and locked the window to the accompaniment of a violent tattoo of knocks on the door. MacAlpine's outraged voice was very loud and clear.

"Open up! Johnny! Open up or I'll break the bloody door in."

Harlow pushed both cameras under the bed. He tore off his black leather jacket and black roll-neck pullover and thrust them both after the cameras. He then took a quick swill of whisky, spilt a little in the palm of his hand and rubbed it over his face.

The door burst open to show MacAlpine's outstretched right leg, the heel of which he'd obviously used against the lock. Both MacAlpine and Dunnet entered, then stood still. Harlow, clad only in shirt and trousers and still wearing his shoes, was stretched out in bed, apparently in an almost coma-like condition. His arm dangled over the side of the bed, his right hand clutching the neck of the whisky bottle. MacAlpine, grim-faced and almost incredulous, approached the bed, bent over Harlow, sniffed in disgust and removed the bottle from Harlow's nerveless hand. He looked at Dunnet, who returned his expressionless glance.

MacAlpine said: "The greatest driver in the world."

"Please, James. You said it yourself. It happens to all of them. Remember? Sooner or later, it happens to them all."

"But Johnny Harlow?"

"Even to Johnny Harlow."

MacAlpine nodded. Both men turned and left the room, closing the broken door behind them. Harlow opened his eyes, rubbed his chin thoughtfully. His hand stopped moving and he sniffed his palm. He wrinkled his nose in distaste.

THREE

▮▮▮▮▮▮▮▮▮▮▮▮▮▮▮▮▮▮▮▮▮▮▮▮▮

As the crowded weeks after the Clermont-Ferrand race rushed by there appeared to be little change in Johnny Harlow. Always a remote, withdrawn and lonely figure, remote and withdrawn he still remained, except that he was now more lonely than ever. In his great days, at the peak of his powers and the height of his fame, he had been a man relaxed to the point of abnormality, his inner self under iron control: and so, in his quietness, he seemed to be now, as aloofly remote and detached as ever, those remarkable eyes—remarkable in the quality of their phenomenal eyesight, not in appearance—as clear and calm and unblinking as ever and the aquiline face quite devoid of expression.

The hands were still now, hands that spoke a man at peace with himself, but it would seem likely that the hands belied and did not bespeak for it seemed equally that he was not at peace with himself and never would be again, for to say that Johnny Harlow's fortunes steadily declined from that day he had killed Jethou and crippled Mary one would be guilty of a sad misuse of the English language. They hadn't declined, they had collapsed with what must have been for him—and most certainly for his great circle of friends, acquaintances and admirers—a complete and shattering finality.

Two weeks after the death of Jethou—and this before his own home British crowd who had come, almost to a man, to forgive him for the dreadful insults and accusations heaped upon him by the French press and to cheer their idol home to victory —he had suffered the indignity, not to say the humiliation, of running off the track in the very first lap. He had caused no damage either to himself or any spectator but his Coronado was a total write-off. As both front tyres had burst it was assumed that at least one of them had gone before the car had left the track: there could not, it was agreed, have been any other explanation for Harlow's abrupt departure into the wilderness. This agreement was not quite universal. Jacobson, predictably, had privately expressed his opinion that the accepted explanation was a very charitable assumption indeed. Jacobson was becoming very attached to the phrase "driver error."

Two weeks after that, at the German Grand Prix —probably the most difficult circuit in Europe but one of which Harlow was an acknowledged master —the air of gloom and despondency that hung like a thundercloud over the Coronado pits was almost palpable enough, almost visible enough to take hold of and push to one side—were it not for the fact that this particular cloud was immovable. The race was over and the last of the Grand Prix cars had vanished to complete the final circuit of the track before coming into their pits.

MacAlpine, looking both despondent and bitter, glanced at Dunnet, who lowered his eyes, bit his lower lip and shook his head. MacAlpine looked away and lost himself in his own private thoughts. Mary sat on a canvas chair close beside them. Her left leg was still in heavy plaster and crutches were propped up against her chair. She held a lap-time note-pad in one hand, a stop watch and pencil in the other. She was gnawing a pencil and her pale face held the expression of one who was pretty close to tears. Behind her stood Jacobson, his two mechanics and Rory. Jacobson's face, if his habitual saturnine expression were excepted, was quite without expression. His mechanics, the red-haired Rafferty twins, wore, as usual, identical expressions, in this case a mixture of resignation and despair: Rory's face registered nothing but a cold contempt.

Rory said: "Eleventh out of twelve finishers! Boy, what a driver. Our world champion—doing his lap of honour, I suppose."

Jacobson looked at him speculatively.

"A month ago he was your idol, Rory."

Rory looked across at his sister. She was still gnawing her pencil, the shoulders were drooped and the tears in her eyes were now unmistakable. Rory looked back at Jacobson and said: "That was a month ago."

A lime-green Coronado swept into the pits, braked and stopped, its crackling exhaust fading away into silence. Nicola Tracchia removed his helmet, produced a large silk handkerchief, wiped his matinee-idol face and started to remove his gloves. He looked, and with reason, particularly pleased with himself, for he had just finished second and that by only a car's length. MacAlpine crossed to him and patted the still-seated Tracchia on the back.

"A magnificent race, Nikki. Your best ever—and on this brute of a course. Your third second place in five times out." He smiled. "You know, I'm beginning to think that we may make a driver of you yet."

Tracchia grinned hugely and climbed from the car.

"Watch me next time out. So far, Nicola Tracchia hasn't really been trying, just trying to improve the performance of those machines our chief mechanic ruins for us between races." He smiled at Jacobson, who grinned back: despite the marked differences in the natures and interests, there was a close affinity between the two men. "Now, when it comes to the Austrian Grand Prix in a couple of weeks—well, I'm sure you can afford a couple of bottles of champagne."

MacAlpine smiled again and it was clear that though the smile did not come easily its reluctance was not directed against Tracchia. In the space of one brief month MacAlpine, even though he still couldn't conceivably be called a thin person, had noticeably lost weight in both body and face, the already trenched lines in the latter seemed to have deepened and it was possible even to imagine an increase in the silver on that magnificent head of hair. It was difficult to imagine that even the precipitous fall from grace of his superstar could have been responsible for so dramatic a change but it was equally difficult to imagine that there could have been any other reason. MacAlpine said:

"Overlooking the fact, aren't we, that there'll be a real live Austrian at the Austrian Grand Prix. Chap called Willi Neubauer. You *have* heard of him?"

Tracchia was unperturbed. "Austrian our Willi may be, but the Austrian Grand Prix is not his circuit. He's never come in better than fourth. I've been second in the last two years." He glanced away as another Coronado entered the pits, then looked back at MacAlpine. "And you know who came in first both times."

"Yes, I know." MacAlpine turned away heavily and approached the other car as Harlow got out, removed his helmet, looked at his car and shook his head. When MacAlpine spoke there was no bitterness nor anger nor accusation in either voice or face, just a faint resignation and despair.

"Well, Johnny, you can't win them all."

Harlow said: "Not with this car I can't."

"Meaning?"

"Loss of power in the higher revs."

Jacobson had approached and his face was still without expression as he heard Harlow's explanation. He said: "From the start?"

"No. Nothing to do with you, Jake, I know that. It was bloody funny. Kept coming and going. At least a dozen times I got full power back. But never for long." He turned away and moodily examined his car again. Jacobson glanced at MacAlpine, who gave him an all but imperceptible nod.

By dusk that evening the race-track was deserted, the last of the crowds and officials gone. MacAlpine, a lonely and brooding figure, his hands thrust deeply in the pockets of his tan gabardine suit, stood at the entrance of the Coronado pits. He wasn't, however, quite as alone as he might justifiably have imagined. In the neighbouring Cagliari pits a figure clad in dark roll-neck pullover and dark leather jacket stood hidden in a shadowed corner. Johnny Harlow had a remarkable capacity for maintaining an absolute stillness and that capacity he was employing to the full at that moment. But apart from those two figures the entire track seemed quite empty of life.

But not of sound. There came the deepening clamour of the sound of a Grand Prix engine and a Coronado, lights on, appeared from the distance, changed down through the gears, slowed right down as it passed the Cagliari pits and came to a halt outside the entrance to the Coronado pits. Jacobson climbed out and removed his helmet.

MacAlpine said: "Well?"

"Damn all the matter with the car." His tone was neutral but his eyes were hard. "Went like a bird. Our Johnny certainly knows how to use his imagination. We've got something more than just driver error here, Mr MacAlpine."

MacAlpine hesitated. The fact that Jacobson had made a perfect lap circuit was no proof of anything one way or another. In the nature of things he would have been unable to drive the Coronado at anything like the speed Harlow had done. Again, the fault may have occurred only when the engine had heated to its maximum and it was unlikely that Jacobson could have reached that in a single lap; finally, those highly bred racing engines, which could cost up to eight thousand pounds, were extraordinarily fickle creatures and quite capable of developing and clearing up their own faults without the hand of man going anywhere near them. Jacobson, inevitably, regarded MacAlpine's silence as either doubt or outright agreement. He said: "Maybe you're coming round to my way of thinking, Mr MacAlpine?"

MacAlpine didn't say whether he was or he wasn't. He said instead: "Just leave the car where she is. We'll send Henry and the two boys down with the transporter to pick it up. Come along. Dinner. I think we've earned it. And a drink. I think we've earned that, too. In fact I don't think I've ever earned so many drinks as I have in the past four weeks."

"I wouldn't disagree with you on that, Mr MacAlpine."

MacAlpine's blue Aston Martin lay parked in the rear of the pits. Both men climbed in and drove off down the track.

Harlow watched the car depart. If he had been disturbed by the conclusions Jacobson had arrived at or MacAlpine's apparent acceptance of them no signs of any such anxiety were reflected in his untroubled face. He waited until the car had disappeared into the gathering darkness, looked round carefully to make sure that he was entirely alone and unobserved, then moved into the back of the Cagliari pits. There he opened a canvas bag he was carrying, produced a flat-based lamplight with a large swivelling head, a hammer, cold chisel and screw-driver and set them on top of the nearest crate. He pressed the switch on the handle of the lamplight and a powerful white beam illuminated the back of the Cagliari pits. A flick on the lever on the base of the swivelling head and the white dazzle was at once replaced by a red muted glow. Harlow took hammer and chisel in hand and set resolutely to work.

Most of the crates and boxes did not, in fact, have to be forced for the esoteric collection of engine and chassis spares inside them could not conceivably have been of any interest to any passing thief: he almost certainly wouldn't have known what to look for and, in the remote event of his so knowing, he would quite certainly have been unable to dispose of them. The few crates that Harlow did have to open he did so carefully, gently and with very little noise.

Harlow spent the minimum of time on his examination, presumably because delay always increased the danger of discovery. He also appeared to know exactly what he was looking for. The contents of some boxes were disposed of with only the most cursory of glances: even the largest of the crates merited no more than a minute's inspection. Within half an hour after beginning the operation he had begun to close all the crates and boxes up again. Those he had been compelled to force open he closed with a cloth-headed hammer to reduce noise to a minimum and leave the least perceptible traces of his passing. When he was finished, he returned his torch and tools to the canvas bag, emerged from the Cagliari pits and walked away into the near darkness. If he was disappointed with the results of his investigation he did not show it: but, then, Harlow rarely showed any emotion.

Fourteen days later Nicola Tracchia achieved what he promised MacAlpine he would achieve—the ambition of his life. He won the Austrian Grand Prix. Harlow, by now predictably, won nothing. Worse, not only did he not finish the race, he hardly even began it, achieving only four more laps than he had in England—and there he had crashed on the first lap.

He had begun well enough. By any standards, even his own, he had made a brilliantly successful start and was leading the field by a clear margin after the end of the fifth lap. Next time round he pulled his Coronado into the pits. As he stepped out of his car he seemed normal enough, with no trace of undue anxiety and nothing even closely resembling a cold sweat. But he had his hands thrust deeply into his overall pockets and his fists were tightly balled: this way you can't tell whether a man's hands are shaking or not. He removed one hand long enough to make a dismissive gesture towards all the pit crew—with the exception of the still chair-borne Mary—and they came hurrying towards him.

"No panic." He shook his head. "And no hurry. Fourth gear's gone." He stood looking out moodily over the track. MacAlpine stared at him closely then looked at Dunnet, who nodded without even appearing to have seen the glance that MacAlpine had directed at him. Dunnet was staring at the clenched hands inside Harlow's pockets.

MacAlpine said: "We'll pull Nikki in. You can have his car."

Harlow didn't answer immediately. There came the sound of an approaching racing engine and Harlow nodded towards the track. The others followed his line of sight. A lime-green Coronado flashed by but still Harlow stared out over the track. At least another fifteen seconds elapsed before the next car, Neubauer's royal blue Cagliari came by. Harlow turned and looked at MacAlpine. Harlow's normally impassive face had come as near as it was possible for it to register a degree of incredulity.

"Pull him in? Good God, Mac, are you mad? Nikki's got fifteen clear seconds now that I'm out. There's no way he can lose. Our Signor Tracchia would never forgive me—or you—if you were to pull him in now. It'll be his first Grand Prix—and the one he most wanted to win."

Harlow turned and walked away as if the matter was settled. Both Mary and Rory watched him go, the former with dull misery in her eyes, the latter with a mixture of triumph and contempt at which he was no pains at all to conceal. MacAlpine hesitated, made as if to speak, then he too turned and walked away, although in a different direction. Dunnet accompanied him. The two men halted in a corner of the pits.

MacAlpine said: "Well?"

Dunnet said: "Well what, James?"

"Please. I don't deserve that from you."

"You mean, did I see what you saw? His hands?"

"He's got the shakes again." MacAlpine made a long pause then sighed and shook his head. "I keep on saying it. It happens to them all. No matter how cool or brave or brilliant—hell, I've said it all before. And when a man has icy calm and iron control like Johnny—well, when the break comes it's liable to be a pretty drastic one."

"And when does the break come?"

"Pretty soon, I think. I'll give him one more Grand Prix."

"Do you know what he's going to do now? Later tonight, rather—he's become very crafty about it."

"I don't think I want to know."

"He's going to hit the bottle."

A voice with a very powerful Glasgow accent said: "The word is that he already has."

Both MacAlpine and Dunnet turned slowly round. Coming out of the shadows of the hut behind was a small man with an incredibly wizened face, whose straggling white moustache contrasted oddly with his monk's tonsure. Even odder was the long, thin and remarkably bent black cigar protruding from one corner of his virtually toothless mouth. His name was Henry, he was the transporter's old driver—long past retiring age—and the cigar was his trademark. It was said that he occasionally ate with the cigar in his mouth.

MacAlpine said without inflection: "Eavesdropping, eh?"

"Eavesdropping!" It was difficult to say whether Henry's tone and expression reflected indignation or incredulity but in either event they were on an Olympian scale. "You know very well that I would never eavesdrop, Mr MacAlpine. I was just listening. There's a difference."

"What did you say just now?"

"I know you heard what I said." Henry was still splendidly unperturbed. "You know that he's driving like a madman and that all the other drivers are getting terrified of him. In fact, they *are* terrified of him. He shouldn't be allowed on a race-track again. The man's shot, you can see that. And in Glasgow, when we say that a man's shot, we mean—"

Dunnet said: "We know what you mean. I thought you were a friend of his, Henry?"

"Aye, I'm all that. Finest gentleman I've ever known, begging the pardon of you two gentlemen. It's because I'm his friend that I don't want him killed—or had up for manslaughter."

MacAlpine said without animosity: "You stick to your job of running the transporter, Henry: I'll stick to mine of running the Coronado team."

Henry nodded and turned away, gravity in his face and a certain carefully controlled degree of outrage in his walk as if to say he'd done his duty, delivered his witch's warning and if that warning were not acted upon the consequences weren't going to be his, Henry's, fault. MacAlpine, his face equally grave, rubbed his cheek thoughtfully and said: "He could be right at that. In fact, I have every reason for thinking he is."

"Is what, James?"

"On the skids. On the rocks. Shot, as Henry would say."

"Shot by whom? By what?"

"Chap called Bacchus, Alexis. The chap that prefers using booze to bullets."

"You have evidence of this?"

"Not so much evidence of his drinking as lack of evidence of his not drinking. Which can be just as damning."

"Sorry, don't follow. Can it be that you have been holding out on me, James?"

MacAlpine nodded and told briefly of his duplicity in the line of duty. It was just after the day that Jethou had died and Harlow had shown his lack of expertise both in pouring and drinking brandy that MacAlpine had first suspected that Harlow had foregone his lifelong abstention from alcohol. There had been, of course, no spectacular drinking bouts, for those would have been automatically responsible for having him banned from the race-tracks of the world: a genius for avoiding company, he just went about it quietly, steadily, persistently and above all secretly, for Harlow always drank alone, almost invariably in out-of-the-way places, usually quite remote, where he stood little or no chance of being discovered. This MacAlpine knew for he had hired what was practically a full-time investigator to follow him but Harlow was either extremely lucky or, aware of what was going on—he was a man of quite remarkable intelligence and must have suspected the possibility of his being followed—extremely astute and skilled in his avoidance of surveillance, for he had been tracked down only three times to sources of supply, small *weinstuben* lost in the forests near the Hockenheim and Nurburgring circuits. Even on those occasions he had been observed to be sipping, delicately and with what appeared to be commendable restraint, a small glass of hock, which was hardly sufficient to blunt even the highly tuned faculties and reactions of a Formula One driver: what made this elusiveness all the more remarkable was that Harlow drove everywhere in his flame-red Ferrari, the most conspicuous car on the roads of Europe. But that he went to such extraordinary—and extraordinarily successful —lengths to escape surveillance was, for MacAlpine, all the circumstantial evidence he required that Harlow's frequent, mysterious and unexplained absences coincided with Harlow's frequent and solitary drinking bouts. MacAlpine finished by saying that a later and more sinister note had crept in: there was now daily and incontrovertible evidence that Harlow had developed a powerful affinity for Scotch.

Dunnet was silent until he saw that MacAlpine apparently had no intention of adding to what he had said. "Evidence?" he said. "What kind of evidence?"

"Olfactory evidence."

Dunnet paused briefly then said: "I've never smelt anything."

MacAlpine said kindly: "That, Alexis, is because you are not capable of smelling anything. You can't smell oil, you can't smell fuel, you can't smell burning tyres. How do you expect to be able to smell Scotch?"

Dunnet inclined his head in acknowledgment. He said: "Have you smelt anything?"

MacAlpine shook his head.

"Well, then."

MacAlpine said: "He avoids me like the plague nowadays—and you know how close Johnny and myself used to be. Whenever he does get close to me he smells powerfully of menthol throat tablets. Doesn't that say something to you?"

"Come off it, James. That's no evidence."

"Perhaps not, but Tracchia, Jacobson and Rory swear to it."

"Oh, brother, are they unbiassed witnesses. If Johnny is forced to step down who's going to be Coronado's number one driver with a good chance of being the next champion? Who but our Nikki. Jacobson and Johnny have never been on good terms and now the relationship is going from bad to worse: Jacobson doesn't like having his cars smashed up and what he likes even less is Harlow's contention that the smashes have nothing to do with him, which brings into question Jacobson's ability to prepare a car thoroughly. As for Rory, well, frankly, he hates Johnny Harlow's guts: partly because of what Johnny did to Mary, partly because she's never allowed the accident to make the slightest difference in her attitude towards him. I'm afraid, James, that your daughter is the only person left on the team who is still totally devoted to Johnny Harlow."

"Yes, I know." MacAlpine was momentarily silent then said dully: "Mary was the first person to tell me."

"Oh, Jesus!" Dunnet looked miserably out on the track and without looking at MacAlpine said: "You've no option now. You have to fire him. For preference, today."

"You're forgetting, Alexis, that you've just learnt this while I've known it for some time. My mind has been made up. One more Grand Prix."

The parking lot, in the fading light, looked like the last resting place of the behemoths of a bygone age. The huge transporters that carried the racing cars, spare parts and portable workshops around Europe, parked, as they were, in a totally haphazard fashion, loomed menacingly out of the gloom. They were completely devoid of life as evinced by the fact that no light showed from any of them. The car park itself was equally deserted except for a figure that had just appeared from out of the gathering dusk and passed through the entrance to the transporter parking lot.

Johnny Harlow made no apparent attempt to

conceal his presence from any chance observer, if any such there had been. Swinging his little canvas bag he made his way diagonally across the parking lot until he brought up at one of the huge behemoths: written large on the side and back was the word FERRARI. He didn't even bother to try the door of the transporter but produced a bunch of curiously shaped keys and had the door open in a matter of a few seconds. He passed inside and closed and locked the door behind him. For five minutes he did nothing other than move from window to window on either side of the transporter checking patiently, continuously, to see if his unauthorised entrance had been observed. It was apparent that it had not been. Satisfied, Harlow withdrew the flashlamp from the canvas bag, switched on the red beam, stooped over the nearest Ferrari racing car and began to examine it minutely.

There were about thirty people in the hotel lobby that evening. Among them were Mary MacAlpine and her brother, Henry and the two red-haired Rafferty twins. The sound level of the conversation was notably high: the hotel had been taken over for the weekend by several of the Grand Prix teams and the racing fraternity is not particularly renowned for its inhibitions. All of them, mainly drivers but with several mechanics, had discarded their workaday clothes and were suitably attired for their evening meal, which was as yet an hour distant. Henry, especially, was exceptionally resplendent in a grey

pinstriped suit with a red rose in his button-hole.
Even his moustache appeared to have been combed.
Mary sat beside him with Rory a few feet away,
reading a magazine, or at least appearing to do so.
Mary sat silently, unsmiling, constantly gripping
and twisting one of the walking sticks to which she
had now graduated. Suddenly, she turned to Henry.

"Where *does* Johnny go each evening. We hardly
ever see him after dinner nowadays."

"Johnny?" Henry adjusted the flower in his button-hole. "No idea, miss. Maybe he prefers his own
company. Maybe he finds the food better elsewhere.
Maybe anything."

Rory still held the magazine before his face.
Clearly however he was not reading for his eyes
were very still. But, at the moment, his whole being
was not in his eyes but in his ears.

Mary said: "Maybe it's not just the food that he
finds better elsewhere."

"Girls, Miss? Johnny Harlow's not interested in
girls." He leered at her in what he probably imagined to be a roguish fashion in keeping with the
gentlemanly splendour of his evening wear. "Except
for a certain you-know-who."

"Don't be such a fool." Mary MacAlpine was not
always milk and roses. "You know what I mean."

"What *do* you mean, miss?"

"Don't be clever with me, Henry."

Henry assumed the sad expression of the continuously misjudged.

"I'm not clever enough to be clever with anybody."

Mary looked at him in cold speculation then abruptly turned away. Rory just as quickly averted his own head. He was looking very thoughtful indeed and the expression superimposed upon the thoughtfulness could hardly be described as pleasant.

Harlow, the hooded red light giving all the illumination he required, probed the depths of a box of spares. Suddenly, he half straightened, cocked his head as if to listen, switched off the torch, went to a side window and peered out. The evening darkness had deepened until it was now almost night, but a yellowish half-moon drifting behind scattered clouds gave just enough light to see by. Two men were heading across the transporter park heading straight towards the Coronado unit, which was less than twenty feet from where Harlow stood watching. There was no difficulty at all in identifying them as MacAlpine and Jacobson. Harlow made his way to the Ferrari transporter's door, unlocked it and cautiously opened it just sufficiently to give him a view of the Coronado transporter's door. MacAlpine was just inserting his key in the lock. MacAlpine said:

"So there's no doubt then. Harlow wasn't imagining things. Fourth gear is stripped."

"Completely."

"So he may be in the clear after all?" There was a note almost of supplication in MacAlpine's voice.

"There's more than one way of stripping a gear." Jacobson's tone offered very little in the way of encouragement.

"There's that, I suppose, there's that. Come on, let's have a look at this damned gear-box."

Both men passed inside and lights came on. Harlow, unusually half-smiling, nodded slowly, closed and gently locked the door and resumed his search. He acted with the same circumspection as he had in the Cagliari pits, forcing open crates and boxes, when this was necessary, with the greatest of care so that they could be closed again to show the absolute minimum of offered violence. He operated with speed and intense concentration, pausing only once at the sound of a noise outside. He checked the source of the noise, saw MacAlpine and Jacobson descending the steps of the Coronado transporter and walk away across the deserted compound. Harlow returned to his work.

FOUR

||||||||||||||||||||||||||||

When Harlow finally returned to the hotel, the lobby, which also served as the bar, was crowded with hardly a seat left vacant and a group of at least a dozen men pressing in close against the bar. Mac-Alpine and Jacobson were sitting at a table with Dunnet. Mary, Henry and Rory were still sitting in the same seats. As Harlow closed the street door behind him, the dinner gong sounded—it was that kind of small country hotel, deliberately so styled, where everyone ate at the same time or not at all. It was a great convenience to management and staff though somewhat less so to the guests.

The guests were rising as Harlow made his way

across the lobby towards the stairs. Nobody greeted him, few even bothered to look at him. MacAlpine, Jacobson and Dunnet ignored him entirely. Rory scowled at him in open contempt. Mary glanced briefly at him, bit her lip and quickly looked away again. Two months previously it would have taken Johnny Harlow five minutes to reach the foot of those stairs. That evening he made it in under ten seconds. If he was in any way dismayed by his reception he hid his concern well. His face was as impassive as that of a wooden Indian's.

In his bedroom, he washed cursorily, combed his hair, crossed to a cupboard, reached for a high shelf, brought down a bottle of Scotch, went into the bathroom, sipped some of the Scotch, swirled it round his mouth then grimaced and spat it out. He left the glass, with its still almost untouched contents, on the basin ledge, returned the bottle to the cupboard and made his way down to the diningroom.

He was the last arrival. A complete stranger entering would have been paid more attention than was accorded to him. Harlow was no longer the person to be seen with. The dining-room was pretty well filled but not to capacity. Most of the tables held four people, a handful held only two. Of the tables that held four people, only three had as few as three people at them. Of the tables for two, only Henry sat alone. Harlow's mouth quirked, so briefly, perhaps even involuntarily, that it could have been more imagined than seen, then, without hesitation, he crossed the dining-room and sat down at Henry's table.

Harlow said: "May I, Henry?"

"Be my guest, Mr Harlow." Henry was cordiality itself, and cordial he remained throughout the meal, talking at length on a wide variety of utterly inconsequential subjects which, try as he might, Harlow found of only minimal interest. Henry's intellectual reach was normally limited in its nature and Harlow found that it was only with considerable difficulty that he could keep up his conversational end against Henry's pedestrian platitudes. To make matters worse he had to listen to Henry's observations from a distance of about six inches, an aesthetic ordeal in itself, as at even a distance of several yards Henry could not, with all charity, have been called photogenic. But Henry appeared to have considered this close-range exchange of intimacies as essential and, in the circumstances, Harlow would have found it hard to disagree with him. The silence in the dining-room that evening was more in the nature of a cathedral hush, one that could not have been attributed to a beatific enjoyment of the food, which was of a standard to earn for the Austrians the most astronomical odds against in the culinary stakes. It was plain to Harlow, as it was plain to all present, that the very fact of his being there had an almost totally inhibitory effect on normal conversation. Henry, consequently, considered it prudent to lower his voice to a graveyard whisper that could not be heard beyond the confines of their table, which in turn necessitated this very personal face-to-face approach. Harlow felt but did not express his profound relief when the meal was over: Henry also suffered from a severe case of halitosis.

Harlow was among the last to rise. He drifted aimlessly into the now again crowded lobby. He stood there in apparent irresolution, quite ignored and glancing idly round. Mary he saw there, and Rory, while at the far end of the lobby MacAlpine was engaged with what appeared to be some form of desultory conversation with Henry.

MacAlpine said: "Well?"

Henry was wearing his self-righteous expression. "Smelled like a distillery, sir."

MacAlpine smiled faintly. "Coming from Glasgow, you should know something about those things. A good job. I owe you an apology, Henry."

Henry inclined his head. "Granted, Mr MacAlpine."

Harlow averted his head from this tableau. He hadn't heard a word of the exchange but then he didn't have to hear it. Suddenly, like a man making up his mind, he headed for the street door. Mary saw him go, looked round to see if she was being observed, came to the apparent conclusion that she wasn't, gathered up her two sticks and limped after him. Rory, in his turn, waited for about ten seconds after his sister's departure then drifted aimlessly towards the door.

Five minutes later Harlow entered a café and took a seat at an empty table where he could keep an eye on the entrance. A pretty young waitress approached, opened her eyes and then smiled charmingly. There were few young people of either sex in Europe who did not recognise Johnny Harlow on sight.

Harlow smiled back. "Tonic and water, please."

The eyes opened even wider. "I beg your pardon, sir."

"Tonic and water."

The waitress, whose opinion of world champion drivers had clearly suffered a sudden revision, brought the drink. He sipped it occasionally, keeping an eye on the entrance door, then frowned as the door opened and Mary, clearly in a very apprehensive mood, entered the café. She saw Harlow at once, limped across the room and sat down at the table.

She said: "Hallo, Johnny," in the voice of one who was far from sure of her reception.

"I must say I'd expected someone else."

"You what?"

"Someone else."

"I don't understand. Who——"

"No matter." Harlow's tone was as brusque as his words. "Who sent you here to spy on me?"

"Spy on you? Spy on you?" She stared at him, the expression on her face one of lack of understanding rather than incredulity. "What on earth can you mean?"

Harlow remained implacable. "Surely you know what the word 'spy' means?"

"Oh, Johnny!" The hurt in the big brown eyes was as unmistakable as that in the voice. "You know I'd never spy on you."

Harlow relented, but only marginally. "Then why are you here?"

"Aren't you pleased just to see me?"

"That's neither here nor there. What are you doing in this café?"

"I was—I was just passing by and—"

"And you saw me and came in." Abruptly he pushed back his chair and rose. "Wait here."

Harlow went to the front door, glanced at it briefly and opened it, stepping just outside. He turned and looked for several seconds back up the way he had come, then turned round and looked down the street. But his interest lay in neither direction, but in a doorway directly across the street. A figure stood there, pushed back deeply into the recess. Without appearing to have noticed him, Harlow re-entered the café, closed the door behind him and returned to his seat.

He said: "Aren't you lucky to have those X-ray eyes. Frosted glass all the way and yet you see me sitting here."

"All right, Johnny." She sounded very weary. "I followed you. I'm worried. I'm dreadfully worried."

"Aren't we all now and again. You should see me out on those race-tracks at times." He paused, then added with apparent inconsequence: "Was Rory still in the hotel when you left."

She blinked her puzzlement. "Yes. Yes he was. I saw him. Just as I was leaving."

"Could he have seen you?"

"That's a funny question."

"I'm a funny fellow. Ask anyone around the race-tracks. Could he have seen you?"

"Well, yes, I suppose he could. Why—why all this concern about Rory?"

"I wouldn't like the poor little lad to be abroad in the streets at night and maybe catch a chill. Or maybe even get mugged." Harlow paused consideringly. "There's a thought, now."

"Oh, stop it, Johnny! Stop it! I know, well I know he can't stand the sight of you, won't even speak to you ever since—ever since—"

"Ever since I crippled you."

"Oh, dear God!" The distress in the face was very real. "He's my brother, Johnny, but he's not me. Can I help it if—look, whatever his grudge, can't you forget it? You're the kindest man in the world, Johnny Harlow—"

"Kindness doesn't pay, Mary."

"You still are. I know you are. Can't you forget it? Can't you forgive him? You're big enough, much more than big enough. Besides, he's only a boy. You're a man. What danger is he to you? What harm can he do you?"

"You should see what harm a dangerous nine-year-old can do in Vietnam when he has a rifle in his hands."

69

She pushed her chair back. The tonelessness in her voice belied the tears in her eyes. She said: "Please forgive me. I shouldn't have bothered you. Goodnight, Johnny."

He laid a gentle hand on her wrist and she made no move to withdraw it, merely sat waiting there with a numbed despair on her face. He said: "Don't go. I just wanted to make sure of something."

"What?"

"Oddly, it doesn't matter any more. Let's forget about Rory. Let's talk of you." He called to the waitress again. "Same again, please."

Mary looked at the freshly filled glass. She said: "What's that? Gin? Vodka?"

"Tonic and water."

"Oh, Johnny!"

"Will you kindly stop 'Oh, Johnnying me.' " It was impossible to tell whether the irritation in his voice was genuine or not. "Now then. You say you are worried—as if you have to tell anyone that, far less me. Let me guess at your worries, Mary. I would say that there are five of them, Rory, yourself, your father, your mother and me." She made as if to speak but he waved her to silence. "You can forget about Rory and his antagonism to me. A month from now and he'll think it was all a bad dream. Then yourself—and don't deny you are worried about our, shall we say, relationship: those things tend to mend but they take time. Then there's your father and mother and, well, me again. I'm about right?"

"You haven't talked to me like this for a long long time."

"Does that mean I'm about right?"

She nodded without speaking.

"Your father. I know he's not looking well, that he's lost weight. I suggest that he's worried about your mother and me, very much in that order."

"My mother," she whispered. "How did you know about that? *Nobody* knows about that except Daddy and me."

"I suspect Alexis Dunnet may know about it, they're very close friends, but I can't be sure. But your father told me, over two months ago. He trusted me, I know, in the days when we were still on speaking terms."

"Please, Johnny."

"Well, I suppose that's better than 'Oh, Johnny.' In spite of all that's passed, I believe he still does. Please don't tell him that I told you because I said I'd tell no-one. Promise?"

"Promise."

"Your father hasn't been very communicative in the past two months. Understandably. And I hardly felt I was in a position to ask him questions. No progress, no trace of her, no message since she left your Marseilles home three months ago?"

"Nothing, nothing." If she'd been the type to wring her hands she'd have done just that. "And she used to phone every day she wasn't with us, write every week and now we—"

"And your father has tried everything?"

"Daddy's a millionaire. Don't *you* think he would have tried everything?"

"I should have thought so. So. You're worried. What can I do?"

Mary briefly drummed her fingers on the table and looked up at him. Her eyes were masked in tears. She said: "You could remove his other main worry."

"Me?"

Mary nodded.

At that precise moment MacAlpine was very actively concerned in investigating his other main worry. He and Dunnet were standing outside an hotel bedroom door, with MacAlpine inserting a key in the lock. Dunnet looked around him apprehensively and said: "I don't think the receptionist believed a word you said."

"Who cares?" MacAlpine turned the key in the lock. "I got Johnny's key, didn't I?"

"And if you hadn't?"

"I'd have kicked his damned door in. I've done it before, haven't I?"

The two men entered, closed and locked the door behind them. Wordlessly and methodically, they began to search Harlow's room, looking equally in the most likely as unlikely places—and in an hotel room the number of places available for concealment to even the most imaginative is very limited. Three minutes and their search was over, a search that had been as rewarding as it was deeply dismaying. The two men gazed down in a brief and almost stunned silence at the haul on Harlow's bed—four full bottles of Scotch and a fifth half full. They looked at each other and Dunnet summed up their feelings in a most succinct fashion indeed.

He said: "Jesus!"

MacAlpine nodded. Unusually for him, he seemed at a total loss for words. He didn't have to say anything for Dunnet to understand and sympathise with his feelings, for the vastly unpleasant dilemma in which MacAlpine now found himself. He had committed himself to giving Harlow his last chance ever and now before him he had all the evidence he would ever require to justify Harlow's instant dismissal.

Dunnet said: "So what do we do?"

"We take that damn poison with us, that's what we do." MacAlpine's eyes were sick, his low voice harsh with strain.

"But he's bound to notice. And at once. From what we know of him now the first thing he'll do on return is head straight for the nearest bottle."

"Who the hell cares what he does or notices? What can he do about it? More importantly, what can he say about it? He's not going to rush down to the desk and shout: 'I'm Johnny Harlow. Someone's just stolen five bottles of Scotch from my room.' He won't be able to do or say a thing."

"Of course he can't. But he'll still know the bottles are gone. What's he going to think about that?"

"Again, who cares what that young dipsomaniac

thinks? Besides, why should it have been us. If we had been responsible, he'd expect the heavens to fall in on him the moment he returns. But they won't. We won't say a word—yet. Could have been any thief posing as a member of the staff. Come to that, it wouldn't have been the first genuine staff member with a leaning towards petty larceny."

"So our little bird won't sing?"

"Our little bird can't. Damn him. Damn him. Damn him."

"Too late, my Mary," Harlow said. "Can't drive no more. Johnny Harlow's on the skids. Ask anyone."

"I don't mean that and you know it. I mean your drinking."

"Me? Drink?" Harlow's face was its usual impassive self. "Who says that?"

"Everybody."

"Everybody's a liar."

As a remark, it was a guaranteed conversation-stopper. A tear fell from Mary's face on to her wrist watch but if Harlow saw it he made no comment. By and by Mary sighed and said quietly: "I give up. I was a fool to try. Johnny, are you coming to the Mayor's reception tonight?"

"No."

"I thought you'd like to take me. Please."

"And make you a martyr? No."

"Why *don't* you come? Every other race driver does."

"I'm not every other driver. I'm Johnny Harlow. I'm a pariah, an outcast. I have a delicate and sensitive nature and I don't like it when nobody speaks to me."

Mary put both her hands on his. "I'll speak to you, Johnny. You know I always will."

"I know." Harlow spoke without either bitterness or irony. "I cripple you for life and you'll always speak to me. Stay away from me, young Mary. I'm poison."

"There are some poisons I could get to like very much indeed."

Harlow squeezed her hand and rose. "Come on. You have to get dressed for this do tonight. I'll see you back to the hotel."

They emerged from the café, Mary using her walking stick with one hand while with the other she clung to Harlow's arm. Harlow, carrying the other stick, had slowed his normal pace to accommodate Mary's limp. As they moved slowly up the street, Rory MacAlpine emerged from the shadows of the recessed doorway opposite the café. He was shivering violently in the cold night air but seemed to be entirely unaware of this. Judging from the look of very considerable satisfaction on his face, Rory had other and more agreeable matters on his mind than the temperature. He crossed the street, followed Harlow and Mary at a discreet distance until he came to the first road junction. He turned right into this and began to run.

By the time he had arrived back at the hotel, he

was no longer shivering but sweating profusely for he had not stopped running all the way. He slowed down to cross the lobby and mount the stairs, went to his room, washed, combed his hair, straightened his tie, spent a few moments in front of his mirror practising his sad but dutiful expression until he thought he had it about right then walked across towards his father's room. He knocked, received some sort of mumbled reply and went inside.

James MacAlpine's suite was, by any odds, the most comfortable in the hotel. As a millionaire, MacAlpine could afford to indulge himself: as both a man and a millionaire he saw no reason why he shouldn't. But MacAlpine wasn't indulging in any indulgence at that moment, nor, as he sat far back in an overstuffed arm-chair, did he appear to be savouring any of the creature comforts surrounding him. He appeared sunk in some deep and private gloom from which he roused himself enough to look up almost apathetically as his son closed the door behind him.

"Well, my boy, what is it? Couldn't it wait until the morning?"

"No, Dad, it couldn't."

"Out with it, then. You can see I'm busy."

"Yes, Dad, I know." Rory's sad but dutiful expression remained in position. "But there's something I felt I had to tell you." He hesitated as if embarrassed at what he was about to say. "It's about Johnny Harlow, Dad."

"Anything you have to say about Harlow will be

treated with the greatest reserve." Despite the words, a degree of interest had crept into MacAlpine's thinning features. "We all know what you think of Harlow."

"Yes, Dad. I thought of that before I came to see you." Rory hesitated again. "You know this thing about Johnny Harlow, Dad? The stories people are telling about his drinking too much."

"Well?" MacAlpine's tone was wholly non-committal. It was with some difficulty that Rory managed to keep his pious expression from slipping: this was going to be much more difficult than he expected.

"It's true. The drinking, I mean. I saw him in a pub tonight."

"Thank you, Rory, you may go." He paused. "Were you in that pub too?"

"Me? Come on, Dad. I was outside. I could see in, though."

"Spying, lad?"

"I was passing by." A curt but injured tone.

MacAlpine waved a hand in dismissal. Rory turned to go, then turned again to face his father.

"Maybe I don't like Johnny Harlow. But I do like Mary. I like her more than any person in the world." MacAlpine nodded, he knew this to be true. "I don't ever want to see her hurt. That's why I came to see you. She was in that pub with Harlow."

"What!" MacAlpine's face had darkened in immediate anger.

"Cut my throat and hope I die."

"You are sure?"

"I *am* sure, Dad. Of course I'm sure. Nothing wrong with my eyes."

"I'm sure there's not," MacAlpine said mechanically. A little, but not much, of the anger had left his eyes. "It's just that I don't want to accept it. Mind you, I don't like spying."

"This wasn't spying, Dad." Rory's indignation could be of a particularly nauseating righteousness at times. "This was detective work. When the good name of the Coronado team is at stake—"

MacAlpine lifted his hand to stop the spate of words and sighed heavily.

"All right, all right, you virtuous little monster. Tell Mary I want her. Now. But don't tell her why."

Five minutes later Rory had been replaced by a Mary who looked simultaneously apprehensive and defiant. She said: "Who told you this?"

"Never mind who told me. Is it true or not?"

"I'm twenty, Daddy." She was very quiet. "I don't have to answer you. I can look after myself."

"Can you? Can you? If I were to throw you off the Coronado team? You've no money and you won't have till I'm dead. You've got no place to go. You've no mother now, at least no mother you can reach. You've no qualifications for anything. Who's going to employ a cripple without qualifications?"

"I would like to hear you say those horrible things to me in front of Johnny Harlow."

"Surprisingly, perhaps, I won't react to that one.

I was just as independent at your age, more so, I guess, and taking a poor view of parental authority." He paused, then went on curiously: "You in love with this fellow?"

"He's not a fellow. He's Johnny Harlow." MacAlpine raised an eyebrow at the intensity in her voice. "As for your question, am I never to be allowed any areas of privacy in my life?"

"All right, all right." MacAlpine sighed. "A deal. If you answer my questions then I'll tell you why I'm asking them. OK?"

She nodded.

"Fine. True or false?"

"If your spies are certain of their facts, Daddy, then why bother asking me?"

"Mind your tongue." The reference to spies had touched MacAlpine to the raw.

"Apologise for saying 'mind your tongue' to me."

"Jesus!" MacAlpine looked at his daughter in an astonishment that was compounded half of irritation, half of admiration. "You must be my daughter. I apologise. Did he drink?"

"Yes."

"What?"

"I don't know. Something clear. He said it was tonic and water."

"And that's the kind of liar you keep company with. Tonic and bloody water! Stay away from him, Mary. If you don't, it's back home to Marseilles for you."

"Why, Daddy? Why? Why? Why?"

"Because God knows I've got enough trouble of my own without having my only daughter tying herself up to an alcoholic with the skids under him."

"Johnny! Alcoholic? Look, Daddy, I know he drinks a little—"

MacAlpine silenced her by the gesture of picking up the phone.

"MacAlpine here. Will you ask Mr Dunnet to come to see me? Yes. Now." He replaced the phone. "I said I'd tell you why I was asking those questions. I didn't want to. But I'm going to have to."

Dunnet entered and closed the door behind him. He had about him the look of a man who was not looking forward too keenly to the next few minutes. After asking Dunnet to sit down MacAlpine said: "Tell her, Alexis, would you, please?"

Dunnet looked even more acutely unhappy. "Must I, James?"

"I'm afraid so. She'd never believe me if I told her what we found in Johnny's room."

Mary looked at each in turn, sheer incredulity in her face. She said: "You were searching Johnny's room."

Dunnet took a deep breath. "With good reason, Mary, and thank God we did. I can still hardly believe it myself. We found five bottles of Scotch hidden in his room. One of them was half empty."

Mary looked at them, stricken. Clearly, she believed them all too well. When MacAlpine spoke, it was very gently.

"I *am* sorry. We all know how fond you are of him. We took the bottles away, incidentally."

"You took the bottles away." Her voice was slow and dull and uncomprehending. "But he'll know. He'll report the theft. There'll be police. There'll be finger-prints—your finger-prints. Then—"

MacAlpine said: "Can you imagine Johnny Harlow ever admitting to anyone in the world that he'd five bottles of Scotch in his room? Run along, girl, and get dressed. We've got to leave for this bloody reception in twenty minutes—without, it seems, your precious Johnny."

She remained seated, her face quite without expression, her unblinking eyes irremovably fixed on MacAlpine's. After a few moments his expression softened and he smiled. He said: "I'm sorry. That was quite uncalled for."

Dunnet held the door while she hobbled from the room. Both men watched her go with pity in their eyes.

FIVE

||||||||||||||||||||||||

To the Grand Prix racing fraternity of the world, as
to seasoned travellers everywhere, an hotel is an
hotel is an hotel, a place to sleep, a place to eat, a
stopover to the next faceless anonymity. The newly
built Villa-Hotel Cessni on the outskirts of Monza,
however, could fairly claim to be an exception to
the truism. Superbly designed, superbly built and
superbly landscaped, its huge airy rooms with their
immaculately designed furniture, their luxurious
bathrooms, splendidly sweeping balconies, sumptu-
ous food and warmth of service, here one would
have thought was the caravanserai nonpareil for the
better-heeled millionaire.

And so it would be, one day, but not yet. The Villa-Hotel Cessni had as yet to establish its clientele, its image, its reputation and, hopefully and eventually, its traditions, and for the achievement of those infinitely desirable ends, the fair uses of publicity, for luxury hotels as for hot-dog stands, could be very sweet indeed. No sport on earth has a more international following and it was with this in mind that the management had deemed it prudent to invite the major Grand Prix teams to accommodate themselves in this palace, for a ludicrously low nominal fee, for the duration of the Italian Grand Prix. Few teams had failed to accept the invitation and fewer still cared to exercise their minds with the philosophical and psychological motivations of the management: all they knew and cared about was that the Villa-Hotel Cessni was infinitely more luxurious and fractionally cheaper than the several Austrian hotels they had so gratefully abandoned only twelve days ago. Next year, it seemed likely, they wouldn't even be allowed to sleep stacked six-deep in the basement: but that was next year.

That Friday evening late in August was warm but by no means warm enough to justify air-conditioning. Nevertheless, the air-conditioning in the lobby of the Villa-Hotel Cessni was operating at the top of its bent making the temperature in that luxuriously appointed haven from the lower classes almost uncomfortably cool. Common sense said that this interior climatic condition was wholly unnecessary: the prestige of an up and coming status symbol said that it was wholly necessary. The management was concerned with prestige to the point of obsession: the air-conditioning remained on. The Cessni was going to be the place to go when the sun rode high.

MacAlpine and Dunnet, sitting side by side but almost concealed from each other's sight by virtue of the imposing construction of the vast velvet-lined arm-chairs in which they reclined rather than sat, had more important things on their minds than a few degrees of temperature hither and yonder. They spoke but seldom and then with a marked lack of animation: they gave the air of those who had precious little to get animated about. Dunnet stirred.

"Our wandering boy is late on the road tonight."

"He has an excuse," MacAlpine said. "At least, I hope to hell he has. One thing, he was always a conscientious workman. He wanted a few more extra laps to adjust the suspension and gear ratios of this new car of his."

Dunnet was gloomy. "It wouldn't have been possible, I suppose, to give it to Tracchia instead?"

"Quite impossible, Alexis, and you know it. The mighty law of protocol. Johnny's not only Coronado's number one, he's still the world's. Our dear sponsors, without which we couldn't very well operate—I could, but I'll be damned if I'll lay out a fortune like that—are highly sensitive people. Sensitive to public opinion, that is. The only reason they paint the names of their damned products on the outside of our cars is that the public will go out and buy those same damned products. They're not benefactors of racing except purely incidentally: they are simply advertisers. An advertiser wants to reach the biggest market. Ninety-nine point repeater nine per cent of that market lies outside the racing world and it doesn't matter a damn if they know nothing about what goes on inside the racing world. It's what they believe that matters. And they believe that Harlow still stands alone. So, Harlow gets the best and newest car. If he doesn't, the public lose their faith in Harlow, in Coronado and in the advertisers, and not necessarily in that order."

"Ah, well. The days of miracles may not yet lie behind us. After all, he hasn't been observed or known to take a drink in the past twelve days. Maybe he's going to surprise us all. And there's only two days to go to the Italian Grand Prix."

"So why did he have those two bottles of Scotch which you removed from his room only an hour ago?"

"I could say he was trying to test his moral fibre but I don't think you would believe it."

"Would you?"

"Frankly, James, no." Dunnet relapsed into another period of gloom from which he emerged to say: "Any word from your agents in the south, James?"

"Nothing. I'm afraid, Alexis, I've just about given up hope. Fourteen weeks now since Marie disappeared. It's too long, it's just too long. Had there been an accident, I would have heard. Had there been foul play, then I'm sure I would have heard. Had it been kidnap and ransom—well, that's ridiculous, of course I would have heard. She's just vanished. Accident, boating—I don't know."

"And we've talked so often about amnesia."

"And I've told you so often, without immodesty, that no-one as well known as Marie MacAlpine, no matter what her mental trouble, could go missing so long without being picked up."

"I know. Mary's taking that pretty badly now, isn't she?"

"Especially in the past twelve days. Harlow. Alexis, we broke her heart—sorry, that's quite unfair—*I* broke her heart in Austria. If I'd known how far she was gone—ah, but I'd no option."

"Taking her to the reception tonight?"

"Yes. I insisted. To take her out of herself, that's what I tell *myself*—or is it just to ease my conscience? Again, I don't know. Maybe I'm making another mistake."

"It seems to me that that young fellow Harlow has a great deal to answer for. And this is his last chance, James? Any more crazy driving, any more fiascos, any more drinking—then it's the chopper? That's it?"

"That's entirely it." MacAlpine nodded in the direction of the revolving entrance doors. "Think we should tell him now?"

Dunnet looked in the direction indicated. Harlow was walking across the Carrara-marbled flags. He was still clad in his customarily immaculate white racing overalls. A young and rather beautiful young girl at the desk smiled at him as he passed by. Harlow flicked her an expressionless glance and the smile froze. He continued on his way across the vast lobby and such is the respect that men accord the gods when they walk the earth that a hundred conversations died as he passed by. Harlow seemed unaware of the presence of any of them, for he looked neither to left nor to right, but it was a safe assumption that those remarkable eyes missed nothing, an assumption borne out by the fact that, apparently without noticing them, he veered towards where MacAlpine and Dunnet sat. MacAlpine said: "No Scotch or menthol, that's for sure. Otherwise, he'd avoid me like the plague."

Harlow stood before them. He said, without any inflection of irony or sarcasm: "Enjoying the quiet evenfall, gentlemen?"

MacAlpine answered. "You could say that. We might enjoy it even more if you could tell us how the new Coronado is coming along."

"Shaping up. Jacobson—for once—agrees with me that a slight alteration in the ratios and the rear suspension is all that's necessary. It'll be all right for Sunday."

"No complaints, then?"

"No. It's a fine car. Best Coronado yet. And fast."

"How fast?"

"I haven't found out yet. But we equalled the lap record the last two times out."

"Well, well." MacAlpine looked at his watch. "Better hurry. We have to leave for the reception in half an hour."

"I'm tired. I'm going to have a shower, two hours sleep then some dinner. I've come here for the Grand Prix, not for mingling with high society."

"You definitely refuse to come?"

"I refused to come last time out too. Setting a precedent, if you like."

"It's obligatory, you know."

"In my vocabulary, obligation and compulsion are not the same things."

"There are three or four very important people present tonight especially just to see you."

"I know."

MacAlpine paused before speaking. "How do you know. Only Alexis and I know."

"Mary told me." Harlow turned and walked away.

"Well." Dunnet pressed his lips tightly together. "The arrogant young bastard. Walking in here to tell us he's just equalled the lap record without even trying. Thing is, I believe him. That's why he stopped by, isn't it."

"To tell me that he's still the best in the business? Partly. Also to tell me to stuff my bloody reception. Also to tell me that he'll speak to Mary whether I like it or not. And the final twist, to let me know that Mary has no secrets from him. Where's that damned daughter of mine?"

88

"This should be interesting to see."

"What should be?"

"To see if you can break a heart twice."

MacAlpine sighed and slumped even further back in his arm-chair. "I suppose you're right, Alexis, I suppose you're right. Mind you, I'd still like to knock their two damned young heads together."

Harlow, clad in a white bath-robe and obviously recently showered, emerged from the bathroom and opened up his wardrobe. He brought out a fresh suit then reached up to a shelf above it. Clearly, he didn't find what he expected to and his eyebrows lifted. He looked in a cupboard with similarly negative results. He stood in the middle of the room, pondering, then smiled widely.

He said softly: "Well, well, well. Here we go again. Clever devils."

From the still-smiling expression on his face, it was clear that Harlow didn't believe his own words. He lifted the mattress, reached under, removed a flat half-bottle of Scotch, examined and replaced it. From there he went into the bathroom, removed the cistern lid, lifted out a bottle of Glenfiddich malt, checked the level—it was about three parts full— replaced it in a certain position and then put the cistern lid back in place. This he left slightly askew. He returned to his bedroom, put on a light grey suit and was just adjusting his tie when he heard the sound of a heavy engine below. He switched out the light, pulled back the curtains, opened his window and peered out cautiously.

A large coach was drawn up outside the hotel entrance and the various drivers, managers, senior mechanics and journalists who were headed for the official reception were filing aboard. Harlow checked to see that all those whose absence that evening he considered highly desirable were among those present, and they were—Dunnet, Tracchia, Neubauer, Jacobson and MacAlpine, the last with a very pale and downcast Mary clinging to his arm. The door closed and the bus moved off into the night.

Five minutes later, Harlow sauntered up to the reception desk. Behind it was the very pretty young girl he'd ignored on the way in. He smiled widely at her—his colleagues wouldn't have believed it—and she, recovering quickly from the shock of seeing the other side of Harlow's nature, smiled in return, almost blushing in embarrassed pleasure. For those outside immediate racing circles, Harlow was still the world's number one.

Harlow said: "Good evening."

"Good evening, Mr Harlow, sir." The smile faded. "I'm afraid you've just missed your bus."

"I have my own private transport."

The smile came back on again. "Of course, Mr Harlow. How silly of me. Your red Ferrari. Is there something—"

"Yes, please. I have four names here—MacAlpine, Neubauer, Tracchia and Jacobson. I wonder if you could give me their room numbers?"

"Certainly, Mr Harlow. But I'm afraid those gentlemen have all just left."

"I know. I *waited* until they had left."

"I don't understand, sir."

"I just want to slip something under their doors. An old pre-race custom."

"You race drivers and your practical jokes." She'd almost certainly never seen a race driver until that evening but that didn't prevent her from giving him a look of roguish understanding. "The numbers you want are 202, 208, 204, and 206."

"That's in the order of the names I gave you?"

"Yes, sir."

"Thank you." Harlow touched a finger to his lips. "Now, not a word."

"Of *course* not, Mr Harlow." She smiled conspiratorially at him as he turned away. Harlow had a sufficiently realistic assessment of his own fame to appreciate that she would talk for months about this brief encounter: just as long as she didn't talk until that weekend was over.

He returned to his own room, took a movie camera from a suitcase, unscrewed its back, carefully scratching the dull metallic black as he did so, removed the plate and pulled out a small miniaturised camera not much larger than a packet of cigarettes. He pocketed this, rescrewed in place the back plate of the movie camera, replaced it in his suitcase and looked thoughtfully at the small canvas bag of tools that lay there. Tonight, he would not require those: where he was going he knew where to find all the tools and flashlights he wanted. He took the bag with him and left the room.

He moved along the corridor to room 202—MacAlpine's room. Unlike MacAlpine, Harlow did not have to resort to devious means to obtain hotel room keys—he had some excellent sets of keys himself. He selected one of these and with the fourth key the door opened. He entered and locked the door behind him.

Having disposed of the canvas bag in the highest and virtually unreachable shelf in a wall wardrobe, Harlow proceeded to search the room thoroughly. Nothing escaped his scrutiny—MacAlpine's clothing, wardrobes, cupboards, suitcases. Finally he came across a locked suitcase, so small as to be almost a brief-case, fastened with locks that were very strong and peculiar indeed. But Harlow had also a set of very small and peculiar keys. Opening the small suitcase presented no difficulty whatsoever.

The interior held a kind of small travelling office, containing as it did a mass of papers, including invoices, receipts, cheque-books and contracts: the owner of the Coronado team obviously served as his own accountant. Harlow ignored everything except an elastic-bound bunch of expired cheque-books. He flipped through those quickly then stopped and stared at the front few pages of one of the cheque-books where all the payments were recorded together. He examined all four recording pages closely, shook his head in evident disbelief, pursed his lips in a soundless whistle, brought out his miniature camera and took eight pictures, two of each page. This done, he returned everything as he had found it and left.

The corridor was deserted. Harlow moved down to 204—Tracchia's room—and used the same key to enter as he had on MacAlpine's door: hotel-room keys have only marginal differences as they have to be to accommodate a master key: what Harlow had was, in fact, a master key.

As Tracchia had considerably fewer possessions than MacAlpine, the search was correspondingly easier. Again Harlow encountered another, but smaller, briefcase, the opening of which again provided him with the minimum of difficulty. There were but few papers inside and Harlow found little of interest among them except a thin book, bound in black and red, of what appeared to be a list of extremely cryptic addresses. Each address, if address it were, was headed by a single letter, followed by two or three wholly indecipherable lines of letters. It could have meant something: it could have meant nothing. Harlow hesitated, obviously in a state of indecision, shrugged, brought out his camera and photographed the pages. He left Tracchia's room in an as immaculate condition as he had left MacAlpine's.

Two minutes later in 208, Harlow, sitting on Neubauer's bed with a brief-case on his lap, was no longer hesitating. The miniature camera clicked busily away: the thin black and red note-book he held in his hand was identical to the one he had found in Tracchia's possession.

From there, Harlow moved on to the last of his four objectives—Jacobson's room. Jacobson, it appeared, was either less discreet or less sophisticated than either Tracchia or Neubauer. He had two bank-books and when Harlow opened them he sat quite still. Jacobson's income, it appeared from them, amounted to at least twenty times as much as he could reasonably expect to earn as a chief mechanic. Inside one of the books was a list of addresses, in plain English, scattered all over Europe. All those details Harlow faithfully recorded on his little camera. He replaced the papers in its case and the case in its original position and was on the point of leaving when he heard footsteps in the corridor. He stood, irresolute, until the footsteps came to a halt outside his door. He pulled a handkerchief from his pocket and was about to use it as a mask when a key turned in the lock. Harlow had time only to move swiftly and silently into a wardrobe, pulling the door quietly to behind him, when the corridor door opened and someone entered the room.

From where Harlow was, all was total darkness. He could hear someone moving around the room but had no idea from the sound as to what the source of the activity might be: for all he could tell someone might have been engaged in exactly the same pursuit as he himself had been a minute ago.

Working purely by feel, he folded his handkerchief cornerwise, adjusted the straight edge to a point just below his eyes and knotted the handkerchief behind the back of his head.

The wardrobe door opened and Harlow was confronted with the spectacle of a portly, middle-aged chambermaid carrying a bolster in her hands—she'd obviously just been changing it for the nighttime pillows. She, in turn, was confronted with the shadowy menacing figure of a man in a white mask. The chambermaid's eyes turned up in her head. Soundlessly, without even as much as a sigh, she swayed and crumpled slowly towards the floor. Harlow stepped out, caught her before she hit the marble tiles and lowered her gently, using the bolster as a pillow. He moved quickly towards the opened corridor door, closed it, removed his handkerchief and proceeded to wipe all the surfaces he had touched, including the top and handle of the brief-case. Finally, he took the telephone off the hook and left it lying on the table. He left, pulling the door to behind him but not quite closing it.

He passed swiftly along the corridor, descended the stairs at a leisurely pace, went to the bar and ordered himself a drink. The barman looked at him in what came close to being open astonishment.

"You said what, sir?"

"Double gin and tonic is what I said."

"Yes, Mr Harlow. Very good, Mr Harlow."

As impassively as he could, the barman prepared the drink, which Harlow took to a wall seat situated between two potted plants. He looked across the lobby with interest. There were some signs of unusual activity at the telephone switchboard, where the girl operator was showing increasing signs of irritation. A light on her board kept flashing on and off but she was obviously having no success in contacting the room number in question. Finally, clearly exasperated, she beckoned a page boy and said something in a low voice. The page boy nodded and crossed the lobby at the properly sedate pace in keeping with the advertised ambience of the Villa-Hotel Cessni.

When he returned, it was at anything but a sedate pace. He ran across the lobby and whispered something urgently to the operator. She left her seat and only seconds later no less a personage than the manager himself appeared and hurried across the lobby. Harlow waited patiently, pretending to sip his drink from time to time. He knew that most people in the lobby were covertly studying him but was unconcerned. From where they sat he was drinking a harmless lemonade or tonic water. The barman, of course, knew better and it was as certain as that night's sundown that one of the first things that MacAlpine would do on his return would be to ask for Johnny Harlow's drink bill, on the convincing enough pretext that it was inconceivable for the champion to put his hand in his pocket for anything.

The manager reappeared moving with most unmanagerial haste, in a sort of disciplined trot, reached the desk and busied himself with the telephone. The entire lobby was now agog with interest and expectation. Their undivided attention had now been transferred from Harlow to the front desk and Harlow took advantage of this to tip the contents of his glass into a potted plant. He rose and sauntered across the lobby as if heading for the front revolving doors. His route brought him past the side of the manager. Harlow broke step.

He said sympathetically: "Trouble?"

"Grave trouble, Mr Harlow. Very grave." The manager had the phone to his ear, obviously waiting for a call to come through, but it was still apparent that he was flattered that Johnny Harlow should take time off to speak to him. "Burglars! Assassins! One of our chambermaids has been most brutally and savagely assaulted."

"Good God! Where?"

"Mr Jacobson's room."

"Jacobson's—but he's only our chief mechanic. He's got nothing worth stealing."

"Aha! Like enough, Mr Harlow. But the burglar wasn't to know that, was he?"

Harlow said anxiously: "I hope she was able to identify her attacker."

"Impossible. All she remembers is a masked giant jumping out of a wardrobe and attacking her. He was carrying a club, she said." He put his hand over the mouthpiece. "Excuse me. The police."

Harlow turned, exhaled a long slow sigh of relief, walked away, passed out through the revolving doors, turned right and then right again, re-entered the hotel through one of the side doors and made his way unobserved back up to his own room. Here he withdrew the sealed film cassette from his miniature camera, replaced it with a fresh one—or one that appeared to be fresh—unscrewed the back of his cine-camera, inserted the miniature and screwed home the back plate of the cine-camera. For good measure, he added a few more scratches to the dulled black metal finish. The original cassette he put in an envelope, wrote on it his name and room number, took it down to the desk, where the more immediate signs of panic appeared to be over, asked that it be put in the safe and returned to his room.

An hour later, Harlow, his more conventional wear now replaced by a navy roll-neck pullover and leather jacket, sat waiting patiently on the edge of his bed. For the second time that night, he heard the sound of a heavy diesel motor outside, for the second time that night he switched off the light, pulled the curtains, opened the window and looked out. The reception party bus had returned. He pulled the curtains to again, switched on the light, removed the flat bottle of Scotch from under the mattress, rinsed his mouth with some of it and left.

He was descending the foot of the stairs as the reception party entered the lobby. Mary, reduced to only one stick now, was on her father's arm but when MacAlpine saw Harlow he handed her to Dunnet. Mary looked at Harlow quietly and steadily but her face didn't say anything.

Harlow made to brush by but MacAlpine barred his way.

MacAlpine said: "The mayor was very vexed and displeased by your absence."

Harlow seemed totally unconcerned by the mayor's reactions. He said: "I'll bet he was the only one."

"You remember you have some practice laps first thing in the morning?"

"I'm the person who has to do them. Is it likely that I would forget?"

Harlow made to move by MacAlpine but the latter blocked his way again.

MacAlpine said: "Where are you going?"

"Out."

"I forbid you——"

"You'll forbid me nothing that isn't in my contract."

Harlow left. Dunnet looked at MacAlpine and sniffed.

"Air *is* a bit thick, isn't it?"

"We missed something," MacAlpine said. "We'd better go and see what it was we missed."

Mary looked at them in turn.

"So you've already searched his room when he was out on the track. And now that his back is turned again you're going to search it again. Despicable. Utterly despicable. You're nothing better than a couple of—a couple of sneak-thieves." She pulled her arm away from Dunnet. "Leave me alone. I can find my own room."

Both men watched her limp across the foyer. Dunnet said complainingly: "Considering the issues involved, life or death issues, if you like, I do consider that a rather unreasonable attitude."

"So is love," MacAlpine sighed. "So is love."

Harlow, descending the hotel steps, brushed by Neubauer and Tracchia. Not only did he not speak to them, for they still remained on courtesy terms, he didn't even appear to see them. Both men turned and looked after Harlow. He was walking with that over-erect, over-stiff posture of the slightly inebriated who are making too good a job of trying to pretend that all is well. Even as they watched, Harlow made one barely perceptible and clearly unpremeditated stagger to one side, but quickly recovered and was back on an over-straight course again. Neubauer and Tracchia exchanged glances, nodded to each other briefly, just once. Neubauer went into the hotel while Tracchia moved off after Harlow.

The earlier warm night air had suddenly begun to chill, the coolness being accompanied by a slight drizzle. This was to Tracchia's advantage. City-dwellers are notoriously averse to anything more than a slight humidity in the atmosphere, and although the Villa-Hotel Cessni was situated in what was really nothing more than a small village, the same urban principle applied: with the first signs of rain the streets began to clear rapidly: the danger of losing Harlow among crowds of people decreased almost to nothingness. The rain increased steadily until finally Tracchia was following Harlow through almost deserted streets. This, of course, increased the chances of detection should Harlow choose to cast a backward glance but it became quickly evident that Harlow had no intention of casting any backward glances: he had about him the fixed and determined air of a man who was heading for a certain objective and backward glances were no part of his forward-looking plans. Tracchia, sensing this, began to move up closer until he was no more than ten yards behind Harlow.

Harlow's behaviour was becoming steadily more erratic. He had lost his ability to pursue a straight line and was beginning to weave noticeably. On one occasion he staggered in against a recessed doorway shop window and Tracchia caught a glimpse of Harlow's reflected face, head shaking and eyes apparently closed. But he pushed himself off and went resolutely if unsteadily on his way. Tracchia closed up even more, his face registering an expression of mingled amusement, contempt and disgust. The expression deepened as Harlow, his condition still deteriorating, lurched round a street corner to his left.

Temporarily out of Tracchia's line of vision, Harlow, all signs of insobriety vanished, moved rapidly into the first darkened doorway round the corner. From a back pocket he withdrew an article not normally carried by racing drivers—a woven leather blackjack with a wrist thong. Harlow slipped the thong over his hand and waited.

He had little enough time to wait. As Tracchia rounded the corner the contempt on his face gave way to consternation when he saw that the ill-lit street ahead was empty. Anxiously, he increased his pace and within half a dozen paces was passing by the shadowed and recessed doorway where Harlow waited.

A Grand Prix driver needs timing, accuracy, and eyesight. All of those Harlow had in super-abundance. Also he was extremely fit. Tracchia lost consciousness instantly. Without as much as a glance at it Harlow stepped over the prostrate body and strode briskly on his way. Only, it wasn't the way he had been going. He retraced his tracks for about a quarter of a mile, turned left and almost at once found himself in the transporter parking lot. It seemed extremely unlikely that Tracchia, when he came to, would have even the slightest idea as to where Harlow had been headed.

Harlow made directly for the nearest transporter. Even through the rain and near darkness the name, in two-feet-high golden letters, was easily distinguishable: CORONADO. He unlocked the door, passed inside and switched on the lights, and very powerful lights they were too, as they had to be for mechanics working on such delicate engineering. Here there was no need for glowing red lights, stealth and secrecy: there was no-one who was going to question Johnny Harlow's rights to be inside his own transporter. Nevertheless, he took the precaution of locking the door from the inside and leaving the key half-turned in the lock so that it couldn't be opened from the outside. Then he used ply to mask the windows so that he couldn't be seen from outside: only then did he make for the tool-rack on the side and select the implements he wanted.

MacAlpine and Dunnet, not for the first time, were illegally in Harlow's room and not feeling too happy about it: not about the illegality but what they had found there. More precisely, they were in Harlow's bathroom. Dunnet had the cistern cover in his hand while MacAlpine held up a dripping bottle of malt whisky. Both men regarded each other, at a momentary loss for words, then Dunnet said: "Resourceful lad is our Johnny. He's probably got a crate hidden under the driving seat of his Coronado. But I think you'd better leave that bottle where you found it."

"Whyever should I? What's the point in that?"

"That way we *may* know his daily consumption. If he can't get it from that bottle he'll sure as hell get it elsewhere—you know his uncanny way of vanishing in that red Ferrari of his. And then we'll never know how much he drinks."

"I suppose so, I suppose so." He looked at the bottle and there was pain in his eyes. "The most gifted driver of our time, perhaps the most gifted driver of all time, and now it's come to this. Why do the gods strike a man like Johnny Harlow down, Alexis? Because he's beginning to walk too close to them."

"Put the bottle back, James."

Only two doors away was another pair of unhappy men, one of them markedly so. Tracchia, from the incessant way in which he massaged the back of his neck, appeared to be in very considerable pain. Neubauer watched him with a mixture of sympathy and anger.

Neubauer said: "Sure it was that bastard Harlow?"

"I'm sure. I've still got my wallet."

"That was careless of him. I think I'll lose my room key and borrow the master."

Tracchia momentarily ceased to massage his aching neck. "What the hell for?"

"You'll see. Stay here."

Neubauer returned within two minutes, a key ring whirling round his finger. He said: "I'm taking the blonde at reception out on Sunday night. I think I'll ask for the keys of the safe next time."

Tracchia said in agonised patience: "Willi, there is a time and a place for comedy."

"Sorry." He opened the door and they passed out into the corridor. It was deserted. Less than ten seconds later they were both inside Harlow's room, the door locked behind them.

Tracchia said: "What happens if Harlow comes along?"

"Who would you rather be? Harlow or us?"

They had spent no more than a minute in searching when Neubauer suddenly said: "You were quite right, Nikki. Our dear friend Johnny *is* just that little bit careless."

He showed Tracchia the cine-camera with the crisscross of scratches round each of the four screws securing the plate at the back, produced a pocket-knife, selected a small screw-driver, removed the plate and extracted the micro-camera. Neubauer then extracted the cassette from the micro-camera and examined it thoughtfully. He said: "We take this?"

Tracchia shook his head and instantly screwed up his face in the agony caused by the thoughtless movement. When he had recovered, he said: "No. He would have known we were here."

Neubauer said: "So there's only one thing for it then?"

Tracchia nodded and again winced in pain. Neubauer lifted off the cover of the cassette, unreeled the film and passed it under a strong desk lamp, then, not without some difficulty, rewound the film, replaced the cover, put the cassette back in the micro-camera and the micro-camera in the cine.

Tracchia said: "This proves nothing. We contact Marseilles?"

Neubauer nodded. Both men left the room.

Harlow had a Coronado pushed back by about a foot. He peered at the section of floor-board revealed, reached for a powerful torch, knelt and examined the floor intently. One of the longitudinal planks appeared to have two transverse lines on it, about fifteen inches apart. Harlow used an oil cloth to rub the front line, whereupon it became evident that the front line was no line at all but a very fine sharp cut. The revealed heads of the two holding nails were bright and clear of any marks. Harlow brought a chisel to bear and the front of the inlet wooden section lifted with surprising ease. He reached down an arm to explore the depth and length of the space beneath. A fractional lifting of the eyebrows expressed some degree of surprise, almost certainly as to the unseen extent of area available. Harlow brought out his arm and touched finger-tips to mouth and nose: there was no perceptible change in his expression. He replaced the board section and gently tapped it into place, using the butt of a chisel on the gleaming nail-heads. With a suitably oiled and dirty cloth he smeared the cuts and nails.

Forty-five minutes had elapsed between the time of Harlow's departure from the Villa-Hotel Cessni and his return there. The vast foyer looked semi-deserted but there must, in fact, have been over a hundred people there, many of them from the official reception party, all of them, probably, waiting to go in for late dinner. The first two people Harlow saw were MacAlpine and Dunnet, sitting alone at a small table with short drinks. Two tables away Mary sat by herself, a soft drink and a magazine in front of her. She didn't give the impression of reading and there was a certain stiff aloofness in her bearing. Harlow wondered towards whom the hostility was directed. Towards himself, likely enough, but on the other hand there had grown up an increasing estrangement between Mary on the one hand and MacAlpine on the other. Of Rory there was no sign. Probably out spying somewhere, Harlow thought.

The three of them caught sight of Harlow at almost the same instant as he saw them. MacAlpine immediately rose to his feet.

"I'd be grateful, Alexis, if you could take Mary in to dinner. I'm going into the dining-room. I'm afraid if I were to stay—"

"It's all right, James. I understand."

Harlow watched the calculated snub of the departing back without expression, an absence of outward feeling that quickly changed to a certain apprehension as he saw Mary bearing down on him. No question now as to whom the unspoken hostility had been directed to. She gave the very distinct impression of having been waiting for him. That bewitching smile that had made her the sweetheart of the race-tracks was, Harlow observed, in marked abeyance. He braced himself for what he knew was going to be a low but correspondingly fierce voice.

"Must you let *everybody* see you like this? And in a *place* like this." Harlow frowned in puzzlement. "You've been at it again."

He said: "That's right. Go ahead. Wound an innocent man's feelings. You have my worded bond—I mean my bonded word—"

"It's disgusting! Sober men don't fall flat on their faces in the street. Look at the state of your clothes, your filthy hands. Go on! Just *look* at yourself."

107

Harlow looked at himself.

"Oh! Aha! Well, sweet dreams, sweet Mary."

He turned towards the stairs, took five steps and halted abruptly when confronted by Dunnet. For a moment the two men looked at each other, faces immobile, then there was an almost imperceptible lift of Dunnet's eyebrow. When Harlow spoke, his voice was very quiet.

He said: "We go now."

"The Coronado?"

"Yes."

"We go now."

SIX

|||||||||||||

Harlow drained his coffee—it was by now his invariable custom to breakfast alone in his bedroom —and crossed to the window. The famed Italian September sun was nowhere to be seen that morning. The overcast was very heavy, but the ground was dry and the visibility excellent, a combination making for ideal race-track conditions. He went into the bathroom, opened the window to its fullest extent, removed the cistern cover, took out the Scotch, turned on the hot water tap and systematically poured half the contents of the bottle into the basin. He returned the bottle to its hiding-place, sprayed the room very heavily with an air-fresh aerosol and left.

He drove alone to the race-track—the passenger seat in his red Ferrari was rarely occupied now—to find Jacobson, his two mechanics and Dunnet already there. He greeted them briefly and in very short order, overalled and helmeted, was sitting in the cockpit of his new Coronado. Jacobson favoured him with his usual grimly despondent look.

He said: "I hope you can give us a good practice lap time today, Johnny."

Harlow said mildly: "I thought I didn't do too badly yesterday. However, one can but try." With his finger on the starter button he glanced at Dunnet. "And where is our worthy employer today? Never known him to miss a practice lap before."

"In the hotel. He has things to attend to."

MacAlpine did, indeed, have things to attend to. What he was attending to at that moment had by this time become almost a routine chore—investigating the current level of Harlow's alcohol supply. As soon as he entered Harlow's bathroom he realised that checking the level of Scotch in the bottle in the cistern was going to be a mere formality: the wide open window and the air heavy with the scent of the aerosol spray made further investigation almost superfluous. However, investigate he did: even although he had been almost certain what to expect, his face still darkened with anger as he held the half-empty bottle up for inspection. He replaced the bottle, left Harlow's room almost at a run, actually ran across the hotel foyer, climbed into his Aston and drove off in a fashion that might well have left the astonished onlookers with the impression that he had mistaken the forecourt of the Villa-Hotel Cessni for the Monza circuit.

MacAlpine was still running when he arrived at the Coronado pits: there he encountered Dunnet, who was just leaving them. MacAlpine was panting heavily. He said: "Where's that young bastard Harlow."

Dunnet did not reply at once. He seemed more concerned with shaking his head slowly from side to side.

"God's sake, man, where's that drunken layabout?" MacAlpine's voice was almost a shout. "He mustn't be allowed anywhere near that damned track."

"There's a lot of other drivers in Monza who would agree with you."

"What's that meant to mean?"

"It means that that drunken layabout has just broken the lap record by two point one seconds." Dunnet continued to shake his head in continued disbelief. "Bloody well incredible."

"Two point one! Two point one! Two point one!" It was MacAlpine's turn to take up the head-shaking. "Impossible. A margin like that? Impossible."

"Ask the time-keepers. He did it twice."

"Jesus!"

"You don't seem as pleased as you might, James."

"Pleased. I'm bloody well terrified. Sure, sure, he's still the best driver in the world—except in actual competition when his nerve goes. But it wasn't driving skill that took him around in that time. It was Dutch courage. Sheer bloody suicidal Dutch courage."

"I don't understand you."

"He'd a half bottle of Scotch inside him, Alexis."

Dunnet stared at him. He said at length: "I don't believe it. I can't believe it. He may have driven like a bat out of hell but he also drove like an angel. Half a bottle of Scotch? He'd have killed himself."

"Perhaps it's as well there was no-one else on the track at the time. He'd have killed them, maybe."

"But—but a whole half bottle!"

"Want to come and have a look in the cistern in his bathroom?"

"No, no. You think I'd ever question your word? It's just that I can't understand it."

"Nor can I, nor can I. And where is our world champion at the moment?"

"Left the track. Says he's through for the day. Says he's got the pole position for tomorrow and if anyone takes it from him he'll just come back and take it away from them again. He's in an uppish sort of mood today, is our Johnny."

"And he never used to talk that way. That's not uppishness, Alexis, it's sheer bloody euphoria dancing on clouds of seventy proof. God Almighty, do I have a problem or do I have a problem."

"You have a problem, James."

On the afternoon of that same Saturday, MacAlpine, had he been in a certain rather shabby little side street in Monza, might well have had justification for thinking that his problems were being doubly or trebly compounded. Two highly undistinguished little cafés faced each other across the narrow street. They had in common the same peeling paint façade, hanging reed curtains, chequered cloth covered sidewalk tables and bare, functional and splendidly uninspired interiors. And both of them, as was so common in cafés of this type, featured high-backed booths facing end on to the street.

Sitting well back from the window in such a booth on the southern and shaded side of the street are Neubauer and Tracchia with untouched drinks in front of them. The drinks are untouched because neither man is interested in them. Their entire interest is concentrated upon the café opposite where, close up to the window and clearly in view, Harlow and Dunnet, glasses in their hands, can be seen engaged in what appears to be earnest discussion across their booth table.

Neubauer said: "Well, now that we've followed them here, Nikki, what do we do now? I mean, you can't lip-read, can you?"

"We wait and see? We play it by ear? I wish to God I could lip-read, Willi. And I'd also like to know why those two have suddenly become so friendly—though they hardly ever speak nowadays in public. And why did they have to come to a little back street like this to talk? We know that Harlow is up to something very funny indeed—the back of my neck still feels half-broken, I could hardly get my damned helmet on today. And if he and Dunnet are so thick then they're both up to the same funny thing. But Dunnet's only a journalist. What can a journalist and a has-been driver be up to?"

"Has-been! Did you see his times this morning?"

"Has-been I said and has-been I meant. You'll see—he'll crack tomorrow just as he's cracked in the last four GP's."

"Yes. Another strange thing. Why is he so good in practice and such a failure in the races themselves?"

"No question. It's common knowledge that Harlow's pretty close to being an alcoholic—I'd say he already is one. All right, so he can drive one fast lap, maybe three. But in an eighty-lap Grand Prix —how can you expect an alco to have the stamina, the reactions, the nerve to last the pace. He'll crack." He looked away from the other café and took a morose sip of his drink. "God, what wouldn't I give to be sitting in the next booth to those two."

Tracchia laid a hand on Neubauer's forearm. "Maybe that won't be necessary, Willi. Maybe we've just found a pair of ears to do our listening for us. Look!"

Neubauer looked. With what appeared to be a considerable degree of stealth and secrecy Rory Mac-Alpine was edging his way into the booth next to the one occupied by Harlow and Dunnet. He was carrying a coloured drink in his hand. When he sat it was with his back to Harlow: physically, they couldn't have been more than a foot apart. Rory adapted a very upright posture, both his back and the back of his head pressed hard against the partition: he was, clearly, listening very intently indeed. He had about him the look of one who was planning a career either as a master spy or double agent. Without question he had a rare talent for observing —and listening—without being observed.

Neubauer said: "What do you think young Mac-Alpine is up to?"

"Here and now?" Tracchia spread his hands. "Anything. The one thing that you can be sure of is that he intends no good to Harlow. I should think he is just trying to get anything he can on Harlow. Just anything. He's a determined young devil—and he hates Harlow. I must say I wouldn't care very much myself to be in his black books."

"So we have an ally, Nikki, yes?"

"I see no reason why not. Let's think up a nice little story to tell him." He peered across the street. "Young Rory doesn't seem too pleased about something."

Rory wasn't. His expression held mixed feelings of vexation, exasperation and perplexity: because of the high back of the booth and the background noise level created by the other patrons of the café, he could catch only snatches of the conversation from the next booth.

Matters weren't helped for Rory by the fact that

Harlow and Dunnet were carrying on this conversation in very low tones indeed. Both of them had tall clear drinks in front of them, both drinks with ice and lemon in them: only one held gin. Dunnet looked consideringly at the tiny film cassette he was cradling in the palm of his hand then slipped it into a safe inside pocket.

"Photographs of code? You're sure?"

"Code for sure. Perhaps even along with some abstruse foreign language. I'm afraid I'm no expert on those matters."

"No more than I am. But we have people who are experts. And the Coronado transporter. You're sure about that too?"

"No question."

"So we've been nursing a viper to our own bosom —if that's the phrase I'm looking for."

"It is a bit embarrassing, isn't it?"

"And no question about Henry having any finger in the pie?"

"Henry?" Harlow shook his head positively. "My life on it."

"Even though, as driver, he's the only person who's with the transporter on every trip it makes?"

"Even though."

"And Henry will have to go?"

"What option do we have?"

"So. Exit Henry—temporarily, though he won't know it: he'll get his old job back. He'll be hurt, of course—but what's one brief hurt to thousands of life-long ones?"

"And if he refuses?"

"I'll have him kidnapped," Dunnet said matter-of-factly. "Or otherwise removed—painlessly, of course. But he'll go along. I've got the doctor's certificate already signed."

"How about medical ethics?"

"The combination of £500 and a genuine certificate of an already existing heart murmur makes medical scruples vanish like a snowflake in the river."

The two men finished their drinks, rose and left. So, after what he presumably regarded as being a suitable safe interval, did Rory. In the café opposite, Neubauer and Tracchia rose hurriedly, walked quickly after Rory and overtook him in half a minute. Rory looked his surprise.

Tracchia said confidentially: "We want to talk to you, Rory. Can you keep a secret?"

Rory looked intrigued but he had a native caution which seldom abandoned him. "What's the secret about?"

"You *are* a suspicious person."

"What's the secret about?"

"Johnny Harlow."

"That's different." Tracchia had Rory's instantaneous and co-operative attention. "Of course I can keep a secret."

Neubauer said: "Well, then, never a whisper. Never one word or you'll ruin everything. You understand?"

"Of course." He hadn't the faintest idea what Neubauer was talking about.

"You've heard of the G.P.D.A.?"

"Course. The Grand Prix Drivers' Association."

"Right. Well, the G.P.D.A. has decided that for the safety of us all, drivers and spectators alike, Harlow must be removed from the Grand Prix roster. We want him taken off all the race-tracks in Europe. You know that he drinks?"

"Who doesn't?"

"He drinks so much that he's become the most dangerous driver in Europe." Neubauer's voice was low-pitched, conspiratorial and totally convincing. "Every other driver is scared to be on the same track as he is. None of us knows when he's going to be the next Jethou."

"You—you mean—"

"He was drunk at the time. That's why a good man dies, Rory—because another man drinks half a bottle of Scotch too many. Would you call that much different from being a murderer?"

"No, by God I wouldn't!"

"So the G.P.D.A. has asked Willi and myself to gather the evidence. About drinking, I mean. Especially before a big race. Will you help us?"

"You have to ask me?"

"We know, boy, we know." Neubauer put his hand on Rory's shoulder, a gesture at once indicative of consolation and understanding. "Mary is our girl, too. You saw Harlow and Mr Dunnet in that café just now. Did Harlow drink?"

"I didn't really see them. I was in the next booth. But I heard Mr Dunnet say something about gin and I saw the waiter bring two tall glasses with what looked like water in them."

"Water!" Tracchia shook his head sadly. "Anyway, that's more like it. Though I can't believe that Dunnet—well, who knows. Did you hear them talk about drink?"

"Mr Dunnet? Is there something wrong with him too?"

Tracchia said evasively, well aware that that was the surest way of arousing Rory's interest: "I don't know anything about Mr Dunnet. About drink, now."

"They spoke in very low voices. I caught something, not much. Not about drink. The only thing I heard was something about changed cassettes—film cassettes—or such-like, something Harlow had given to Mr Dunnet. Didn't make any kind of sense to me."

Tracchia said: "That hardly concerns us. But the rest, yes. Keep your eyes and ears open, will you?"

Rory, carefully concealing his new-found sense of self-importance, nodded man to man and walked away. Neubauer and Tracchia looked at each other with fury in their faces, a fury, clearly, that was not directed at each other.

Through tightly clenched teeth Tracchia said: "The crafty bastard! He's switched cassettes on us. That was a dud we destroyed."

On the evening of that same day Dunnet and Henry sat in a remote corner of the lobby in the Villa-Hotel Cessni. Dunnet wore his usual near-inscrutable expression. Henry looked somewhat stunned although it was clear that his native shrewdness was hard at work making a reassessment of an existing situation and a readjustment to a developing one. He tried hard not to look cunning. He said: "You certainly do know how to lay it on the line, don't you, Mr Dunnet?" The tone of respectful admiration for a higher intellect was perfectly done: Dunnet remained totally unmoved.

"If by laying it on the line, Henry, you mean putting it as briefly and clearly as possible, then, yes, I have laid it on the line. Yes or no?"

"Jesus, Mr Dunnet, you don't give a man much time to think, do you?"

Dunnet said patiently: "This hardly calls for thought, Henry. A simple yes or no. Take it or leave it."

Henry kept his cunning look under wraps. "And if I leave it?"

"We'll cross that bridge when we come to it."

Henry looked distinctly uneasy. "I don't know if I like the sound of that, Mr Dunnet."

"How does it sound to you, Henry?"

"I mean, well, you aren't blackmailing me or threatening me or something like that?"

Dunnet had the air of a man counting up to ten. "You make me say it, Henry. You're talking rubbish. How can one blackmail a man who leads the